BIG

SHOT

BIG SHOT

by M. L. Shochet

ISBN: 9798550352496

DEDICATED TO MY FAMILY

AND DEDICATED TO ROBERT HORRY, CHRIS PAUL, AND ANYONE WHO HAS EVER STARTED THE GAME ON THE BENCH

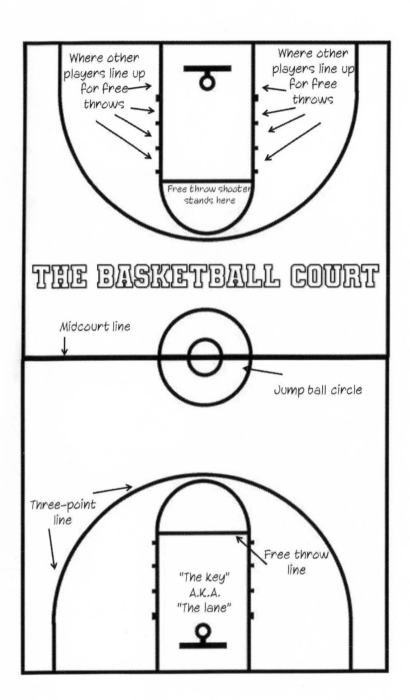

THE BASKETBALL COURT

Where other players line up for free throws →

Where other players line up for free throws ←

Free throw shooter stands here

Midcourt line ↓

Jump ball circle

Three-point line

"The key"
A.K.A.
"The lane"

Free throw line

CHAPTER 1

I couldn't believe it.

I just *couldn't* believe it!

From the time I was six years-old, I, Ben Taylor, was the best basketball player in my class. In fact, I was the only one who was able to shoot the ball into a ten-foot basket. And as I got older, I was always the one picked first for recess games, and I was always one of the best players of my recreation league basketball team. The starting point guard, of course.

I'm not necessarily the fastest guy around, but I work on my fundamentals. Every day after school, I shoot and dribble outside for at least an hour. I work on set shots, jump shots, free throws, you name it.

I'm a good defender, too. I pride myself on keeping my opponent to a minimum of points.

And now?

Now I'm in seventh grade, and it's our school team's first basketball game of the season. And for the first time in my life, I'm a backup.

This year, there is a new point guard on our team, the Ridgeview Eagles. His name is Gerald, and he moved in this past summer from out of town. I have to admit, he's good. We had been competing for the starting point guard spot since team practices had started in late fall.

Whenever we asked, Coach Jones told us that he hadn't yet made his decision on who would be the starter. Just last week, Coach Jones had told us the rest of the starting lineup, but said that he would have to let us know on game day who would be the starting point guard. Gerald is good, sure, but I never believed that he would actually get the starting spot.

And now? Now?

Now I'm sitting on the bench, watching the team play the first quarter of our first game without me.

CHAPTER 2

Just fifteen minutes before, during layup drills, Coach Jones had taken us both over to the bench to speak with us privately.

"Listen, guys," he had said, "You both are really great players, and have both truly earned your spot on this team. There can only be one starting point guard, though. It was a really tough decision, but I have decided to make Gerald the starter. Nothing against you, Ben, but Gerald's just a little bigger and stronger." Coach paused for a second, then concluded, "Okay, go back out there and finish warm-ups, guys."

I watched as Gerald ran back out to the team and said something I couldn't hear to some of the guys. They gave him high-fives before walking back into the layup lines.

I felt warm all over, had a sick feeling in my stomach, and my head was throbbing. I needed to speak to Coach Jones right away.

"Coach?" I asked, with a tone that wasn't as polite as it should have been.

"Yes, Ben?" Coach responded innocently, as if he hadn't just surprised me with terrible news right before the first game of the season.

I stared down at the gym floor and paused for a second, before I looked up again and said, "You know, this is the first time in my life that I have been made a backup. Why didn't you choose me to be the starter? I've always been a starter."

"I know, Ben," Coach said, looking me in the eyes, which were now tearing up. "And your fundamentals and court awareness are really great. It's really nothing against you. Gerald's just a little bigger, stronger, and faster, which makes him harder to stop on the offensive end. But don't worry, Ben. Even though Gerald's officially the starter, you're going to get playing time, also."

The truth is that Gerald is more than just a little bigger than I am. The last time I measured myself, I was four feet, seven and three-quarters inches tall, which makes me the shortest guy on the team. Gerald must be almost six feet tall, and he looms over me when we stand together. And he has real muscles, too, while I'm much skinnier. It's true that his size and strength do give him an advantage, but I wasn't ready to give up trying to change Coach's mind.

"But maybe we could *both* start, and someone else could sit on the bench," I said to Coach Jones.

"I thought about that also, Ben," Coach responded, "but I don't think there's another player you could replace that would leave our starting lineup with the pieces that it needs. It's going to be okay, Ben. You're going to get your time to play and contribute as well. Besides, it's what's best for the team that's important. Right?"

"Right," I said meekly, feeling discouraged. Coach was of course right that what is best for the team is our first priority, even if it means me losing my starting spot. But that doesn't mean that it doesn't still hurt for me to start the game on the bench. And besides, what if Coach isn't right that the team is best off with me on the bench?

CHAPTER 3

As Coach Jones walked away, I thought about our five starting lineup positions. Maybe there was someone I could replace...

Obviously, Gerald Moore is our new starting point guard. Tall, strong and fast, his primary responsibilities on the court are to take the ball up the court, start our offensive plays, and make good passes. As Coach had mentioned, he also has the ability to drive through the crowded lane and score.

William Lee is our shooting guard. William is an inch or two taller than I am, super quick, and specializes in scoring. He doesn't excel in running the offense like a point guard, but when he catches the ball, he is a threat to score from anywhere on the court. While William himself isn't our best defender, he can dribble past almost any opposing defender, can quickly catch and shoot, and has the most accurate 3-point shot on the team. I guess I couldn't replace our biggest scoring threat. Besides, William is my best friend, and I wouldn't be able to bring myself to take away his starting spot.

Michael Lopez is our small forward. Lopez is about 8 inches taller than I am, is a good defender and rebounder, and though he isn't one of our primary offensive weapons, can both drive to the basket and score on mid-range shots. At my size, I definitely couldn't rebound or drive the lane like Michael could.

At power forward, we have Josh Martin, and at center, John Green. Both guys are close to six feet tall and are much stronger than I am. Unlike the guards, their job is to play on the inside on offense and defense, trying to score up close and getting tough rebounds against similarly-sized opponents. With my size, there is no way I can replace one of them.

To my dismay, I realized that Coach was probably right. I half-heartedly jogged back onto the court to join the rest of the team for the last few minutes of warm-up drills.

William Lee, my best friend, came up behind me in the layup line and patted me on my right shoulder.

I turned my head back a little toward him and said, "Hey William, did you hear the news?" I tried to smile, so I wouldn't start crying.

"Yeah, I heard that Gerald got the starting spot. It's gonna be okay, Ben. You'll still get your chance to show how great you are," William said.

"Thanks, William," I said, only half-believing him, and turned around to catch the ball as I moved up in the line.

It was now my turn in the layup line. I dribbled toward the basket, jumped up off my inside foot, extended my right hand to gently shoot the ball off the glass backboard, and watched as the ball hit the backboard and the left side of the rim before bouncing out. I caught the rebound and stood for a second, before passing the ball to the opposite line and running to take my place in the back of that line. I was shaking my head. I had missed a layup on my strong side. Me, Ben Taylor, who practices layups every day and never misses an open layup. But did it even matter? The team hardly needed me anymore, it seemed.

Shaking my head again as I sat on the bench during the first ten minutes of our game against the Sharks, I felt even worse. Watching the game, it was obvious that the team didn't need me at all. Gerald really *was* good. He had already scored eight points of his own and assisted on several other field goals. Our team was winning 20-8, with a quarter of the game already in the books, and I hadn't even stepped on the floor.

Suddenly, I heard Coach's voice call out, "Ben, Allen, Kevin! Get ready! You guys are subbing in at the next whistle. Gerald, Michael and John are coming out."

Subbing in? The words sounded so strange to my ears. I stood up, stretched a little, and tucked in my shirt, as I waited at the scorekeeper's table for the next whistle.

Less than a minute later, Josh, our power forward, tried to go in for a layup and was hit on the arm by one of the Sharks. The referee blew his whistle to call the foul.

"Foul, Blue, Number 24. Two shots," the referee yelled to the scorer's table.

The referee blew his whistle again and gestured to us to come onto the court. We ran onto the court, calling out the names of the players we were replacing. I called Gerald's name and gave him a high-five as he jogged off the court and passed me.

I was finally in! It was time to prove that I deserved to have the starting spot.

CHAPTER 4

I stood in my spot on the left side of the court, behind the three- point line, while most of the other players finished lining up alongside the key, and Josh Martin stepped up to the free throw line to take his shots. As I waited for Josh to get the ball from the ref and take his first shot, I began to survey the court.

I was the point guard on the floor for our team, and William, who had started the game, was the shooting guard alongside me. I flashed a smile to William, who smiled back at me. Allen Walker, who could play at either guard or forward, had just come into the game to play the small forward position. Josh Martin, about to shoot free throws, was still in the game as the power forward, and Kevin Levine had subbed in for John Green at center.

Josh shot his first free throw, which hit the back of the rim and bounced out.

"That's okay, Josh! Get the second one!" Coach Jones called out from the bench.

The opposing point guard on the Sharks was wearing number 22. I would be guarding him on defense. While he was supposed to be one of their best players, he didn't seem so intimidating to me. He is only a little taller than I am, so size wasn't an issue. Also, he had been running up and down the court since the start of the game, and I had just entered with fresh legs. I was confident I would be able to keep up with him.

Josh made his second free throw shot, and we all ran back on defense. I bent my knees, leaned a little on the balls of my feet, and crouched into a defensive stance, waiting just behind the half-court circle as Number 22 brought the ball up the court.

He sure looks calm, considering his team is losing by thirteen points, I thought to myself. *Maybe a little too calm. Let's see if I can catch him off guard and steal the ball away. That would show Coach that I deserve to play.*

As Number 22 crossed over midcourt, I reached with my left hand toward his right side to poke the ball loose. I was too slow. Number 22 did a crossover dribble and drove to his left. As he made the move, he bumped my right shoulder, which sent me falling to the floor, and him stumbling a few steps to the side.

FWEET!

The referee's whistle blew, stopping the play. My feet weren't set when Number 22 bumped me, so the ref was definitely calling a foul on me.

"Blocking foul, Gold, Number 3," called the referee to the scorer's table.

That was me, alright. I always wore number 3, after my favorite player, Chris Paul. He was my favorite since I started watching basketball, even before I started playing. His style of play was the one I tried most to imitate.

Okay, I guess I'm being a little too aggressive, I thought to myself. *Let me just play my normal game.*

The Sharks passed the ball in to Number 22 again, and instead of reaching for a steal, I just played my normal, shutdown defense. The guard tried to make a move, but I was quicker. I beat him to the spot, and he couldn't get past me. He passed the ball to one of his forwards, who took a guarded mid-range shot and missed.

Kevin Levine leapt, caught the rebound above his head, and quickly passed it to me. I turned my head up court and saw Allen Walker starting to sprint up the right side, unguarded. I threw a strong chest pass in his direction. It bounced once before Allen caught it in stride, dribbled it once, and went up for the layup. The ball bounced lightly off the backboard and fell through the hoop. Two points!

As Allen ran back to the rest of us on defense, I heard Coach Jones yelling from the bench, "Attaway, Allen! Great finish! Nice pass, Ben! Good rebound, Kevin! Keep it up!"

It felt great to make the assist to Allen, and also great to hear Coach cheering for us on the sideline.

Alright, here we go, I thought to myself, as Number 22 brought the ball up the court. *Let's stop them again.*

Number 22 passed the ball quickly to his shooting guard, then ran, planted his feet, and stood firmly right to William Lee on the right side. I immediately recognized what was happening. Number 22 was trying to set a pick on William, blocking him so that the shooting guard could dribble around William. Then he'd be open to take a shot or drive to the basket.

In situations like these, we have two main options: either William and I can switch the players we are guarding, or stay with them and let William try to stay with his man and fight through the pick. Each method has its strengths and weaknesses.

Since we have to both know what is going on, it's important for us to communicate verbally. Otherwise, William might think we are switching while I think he's trying to stay with his man, and then we would end up with his man left unguarded.

As the shooting guard made a quick move to go left around the pick and evade William, I quickly called out, "Switch!"

I immediately stepped up to guard the shooting guard, slowing him down. Stopped, he turned left and fired a pass back to Number 22, who was now guarded by William.

Number 22 made a sharp move to his left, then did a crossover dribble to his right side, catching William off-balance. Number 22 drove to the middle of the lane and shot a running floater over Kevin Levine, who had tried to come up and stop him. The ball bounced off the middle of the backboard and went in. Two points for the Sharks.

Josh Martin picked up the ball off the floor, ran to the baseline, and passed the ball inbounds to me to bring the ball up the court.

Hm, I thought to myself as I dribbled up the court. *Maybe they were planning that the whole time, to get me away from guarding Number 22. If they try that again, I'm not going to call a switch.*

I brought the ball to the top of the key and passed left to Kevin, who was standing on the right elbow. Kevin caught it and passed it up to William, standing at about the three-point line, who passed it down to Josh Martin. Josh turned his back to the basket, and dribbled backward twice in the direction of the hoop. Josh's defender stood strongly behind him, making it difficult for Josh to advance.

Josh turned, and made a move like he was going to shoot. He then quickly passed the ball back out to William, who fired a three-pointer as his man jumped out at him. My teammates, not relying on William to make the shot, immediately ran in for the rebound. I took a few steps back in order to get back on defense more quickly in case William missed.

Sure enough, the ball clanged against the back rim and bounced a long way, in front of me to my left, but out of my reach. Number 22 grabbed the ball and started streaking up the court toward me. Out of the corner of my eye, I saw another blue jersey start to run down the other side of the court, as they tried to create a 2-on-1 fast break. I turned and ran back to set up to try to stop the two players by myself.

Standing a few steps behind the foul line, I tried to position myself between Number 22 and where I thought the other player would go, so that Number 22 would not be able to pass the ball to his teammate. Number 22 kept dribbling up the court, and as he got just past the foul line, I made my move, charging toward him, but still sort of blocking his passing lane to his teammate. Number 22 dribbled to the outside and kept driving ahead for a layup. I jumped when he did, extended my hand out to block the ball, and...

...missed, and slapping him on the wrist instead.

FWEET!

The referee's whistle blew again to call another foul on me. Number 22's shot, altered by my foul, fell short of the basket.

The referee held his right hand up with his fist clenched as he called out, "Personal Foul, number 3. Two shots."

I had stopped the fast break, but that was my second foul. Three more in the game and I would foul out and be disqualified from playing in the rest of the game.

CHAPTER 5

Since I had fouled Number 22 while he was trying to shoot, he would have the chance to take two free throws.

Number 22 stood at the free throw line, and most of the players from both teams stood around the edges of the key, so that they would be ready to get a rebound if Number 22 missed his second shot.

William and I, the guards, stood behind the shooter on each side of the three point line. We weren't good rebounders, anyway, and were staying back in order to get a head start on a fast break in case our team got the rebound.

While everyone was getting set up in their positions, the Sharks' shooting guard walked up to me and started talking.

"Hey, isn't your name Ben?" he asked.

17

"Yeah," I said.

"Weren't you the starting point guard for your team last year? You were pretty good, from what I remember," he continued.

Wow, way to rub it in, I thought.

"I used to start, yeah," I told my opponent.

"The new guy seems really good," said the Blue guard. "Great for your team, but tough break for you, man. Sorry."

Wow, way to rub it in even more.

I just nodded and tried to look away. If this guy was trying to make me feel better, he was doing a terrible job at it.

Looking back to the free throw line, I saw Number 22 swish his first free throw through the hoop, adding a point to his team's score. His teammates and coach clapped for him.

FWEET!

I heard the referee's whistle to signal a substitution, and then I heard Gerald call out from behind me, "Ben, I'm in for you!"

I couldn't believe it! I had just gotten in the game a few minutes ago, and now I was being taken out again?!

I turned toward Gerald and asked him in a low voice, "You sure? I just got in!"

Gerald nodded his head and said, "Sorry, man. Coach's orders."

I sat down on the bench alongside William and Josh Martin, who had also just come out of the game, and looked at the game clock, which now read 1:57. Only one minute and fifty-seven

18

seconds left in the first half. Each half was twenty minutes long, and I had entered the game when there were a little more than five minutes left in the half. Doing a quick calculation in my head, I realized I had been in the game for barely more than three minutes! I hung my head down and stared at the floor. This was so different from last year.

In the meantime, Number 22 had made his second foul shot, and Gerald started taking the ball up court for our team to start our offense.

Coach walked over to me on the bench during the action and rested his hand gently on my shoulder for a second before speaking.

"Sorry, Ben. You picked up two quick fouls out there, and we don't want you to foul out, in case we need you later in the game," Coach Jones said.

I understood my coach's explanation, but it didn't make me feel any better. I kept staring at the floor, trying not to cry.

CHAPTER 6

The first half concluded with a loud buzz from the scorer's table, and I looked up at the scoreboard. There must have been more scoring while I had my head down, because our team was up by even more, 30-16.

No thanks to me, I thought.

Everyone went to the bench to get their water bottles and listen to Coach speak for a few minutes, while they caught their breath before the start of the second half. Coach was standing, and the players all sat on the long bench, facing him. I personally didn't have much of a need to recover, as I had barely been in the game. In fact, considering that Allen Walker and Kevin Levine had stayed in the game until the end of the first half, I had played the shortest amount of anyone on the team.

Coach Jones congratulated us on what we did well and reminded us to not let our guard down. We wouldn't want the Sharks to go on a run and get back into the game.

"Box out and crash the boards," Coach said, as he always did, reminding us to get into good position for rebounds, and to rebound aggressively.

"Keep that ball moving on offense. Let's just keep playing our game, guys. Everyone's doing great."

Yeah, except for me.

"Okay, here's the lineup to start the second half: Ben Taylor is starting at point guard, Allen Walker is the shooting guard, Michael Lopez is still in at small forward, Kevin's in at power forward, and John Green is our center. Gerald, William and Josh are starting on the bench, but we'll get you guys in soon."

I was excited to start the second half, even though I realized full well that Coach always put in the backups to start the second half. It was sort of a fresh start, and another chance for me to make a positive mark on the game. I hopped a little in place and moved my arms a bit to warm them up.

"Go get 'em, Ben," William said to me, and gave me a fist bump.

FWEET!

The referee whistled to signal the end of halftime, and stood at the baseline, waiting to hand the ball to a Sharks player to pass it inbounds.

Since our team had won the opening tip-off, the Sharks started with the ball. With Number 22 on the bench to start the second half, Number 16 brought the ball up the court. I met him just beyond midcourt in my defensive stance. He tried to dribble around me to the right and then the left, but I stopped him both times. Number 16 turned away from me and passed it to his shooting guard, who had come up near midcourt to help him. Then, Number 16 surprised me by bolting toward the basket, obviously hoping for a pass back from his teammate. I ran after him. Sure enough, the shooting guard threw a strong, over-the-head pass in his direction.

I stuck my arm out in the direction of the ball, and the ball hit my hand, then my leg, which accidentally kicked it off the court, out of bounds on the sideline.

FWEET!

"Out of bounds! Blue ball!" the referee said, pointing in the direction of the Sharks' basket.

As the referee handed the ball to the Sharks forward standing out of bounds so that he could pass it in, I took a few steps away from Number 16, who was standing in the center of the court at the three point line, what we call "the top of the key."

Seeing his teammate so open, the Sharks forward inbounded the ball with a soft pass to Number 16, and I seized the opportunity to jump in front of my opponent and snatch the ball from the air. I immediately began sprinting down the court toward our basket, with no one in front of me.

As I neared the basket, I slowed down slightly as I prepared to jump and lay the ball in.

I leapt off my left foot, extended my right arm, and...*slam!*

Someone crashed into me from behind, knocking me down to the floor and making my shot miss wildly.

FWEET!

Ouch, I thought to myself, laying on the floor for a few seconds. *Guess I shouldn't have slowed down. Coach always tells me not to...*

"Personal Foul, Blue Number 16! Two shots!" The referee shouted.

I got up off the floor and looked back at Number 16, who was now staring at me. He looked like a mean guy. Not scary or anything. Just mean. Maybe he was frustrated his team was losing so badly. Either way, I wasn't scared of him, nor was I going to let him think that he intimidated me. I walked to the foul line, staring right back at him.

I stood behind the free throw line as the Eagles and the Sharks players lined up at the spots along the sides of the key. The referee bounced me the ball. I followed the same free throw routine that Chris Paul always does. Dribble the ball once. Catch it. Adjust my hands on the ball. Bend my knees slightly and shoot.

Swish!

"Nice, Ben!" Coach called out from the bench after my first shot, clapping a few times.

I caught the ball again from the referee and went into the same routine. Dribble the ball once. Catch it. Adjust my hands on the ball. Bend my knees slightly and shoot.

Swish!

As we continued playing for the next few minutes, everything felt so good and normal again. True, I didn't have all the starters playing alongside me, especially my best friend William, but I was still able to get into a groove on offense and play good defense.

The Sharks called timeout to regroup, and I looked up at the scoreboard. We were winning, big time. The score was 42-20, with fifteen minutes still left to play. It was shaping up to be a real blowout.

In our huddle, Coach Jones congratulated the players on a job well done so far and said that the same players that had been on the floor would stay in the game.

Yes! I thought. *I'm finally going to get some decent playing time.*

Coach reminded us again us not to let our guard down, though, and stressed that the game wasn't over yet.

The Sharks came back out on the floor with all five of their starters. That meant that I would be covering Number 22 again, the same guy who had given me some trouble before.

It was likely that the Sharks had called timeout and brought back all their starters into the game in order to make one last strong push to catch up, before the game was totally out of reach. We could expect their very best effort in the minutes to come.

CHAPTER 7

With their chances of winning quickly fading, I fully expected the Sharks to ramp up their level of intensity. I imagine they'd play aggressive defense, something like a full-court press. Maybe they'd try to trap us and steal the ball away in order to make up some quick points. Those types of aggressive defenses are risky, but do have the potential to help teams score points in a hurry.

To my surprise, the Sharks just continued playing as if the score were tied, instead of us leading by 22 points. That was just fine with me—the lower the pressure, the better.

While I stayed on the floor for the next few minutes, both teams played about even, and I managed to throw a few good passes to help set up some of my team's field goals. With twelve minutes left on the play clock, I was taken out of the game, along with the other reserves, in order to allow the starters to finish the game.

I watched the rest of the game from the bench as our team coasted to victory against the Sharks. When the final buzzer had sounded, the Eagles had won by a huge margin, 59-40, and everyone was smiling, even me. Winning has a certain magic to it that can lift downtrodden spirits. Moreover, the Eagles seemed really strong this year, and a big win like this was a good way to begin our season.

After we shook hands with the other team and wished them "good game", Coach Jones called us back to the bench to give us some final words before sending us home.

"I'm really impressed with how you guys played today. Really good effort from beginning to end, Eagles. You moved the ball well on offense and played solid defense the whole game. A truly great job all around. If we can keep this up, I think we'll have a good shot at going far in the playoffs this year."

Everyone smiled when Coach said that last line. Coach Jones's conservative philosophy was always, "One game at a time," so it was a surprise to hear him predict a deep playoff run after the very first game of the season. Coach hadn't finished speaking, though.

"And Gerald, wow! You really showed that you earned the starting spot with your performance today. Great play on both sides of the ball. We're so fortunate to have you on our team," Coach continued.

Listening to Coach Jones had taken me on an emotional ride, from excitement to dejection. My disappointment during the earlier parts of the game had been soothed by the playing time I had received in the second half, as well as the joy of seeing our team win so thoroughly. Coach had just given our team so much praise after a good game. But when he singled out Gerald in such a complimentary way, it reminded me of what I had used to mean to our team, and how much things had changed.

I stared at the ground as I listened to Coach remind the team about our practice after school this coming Tuesday. It was still hard for me to swallow the thought that I was going to be a backup from now on.

I wasn't ready to give up hope yet, though. If my father had taught me anything, it was that I could achieve anything I put my mind to. My next order of business would be to speak to my Dad about a plan for earning my starting spot back.

CHAPTER 8

"Give it up, Ben," my Dad said. "You're not going to have the starting spot this year. Just accept it and move on."

I couldn't believe my ears. My mother and father and I had been speaking for half an hour in our kitchen about losing my starting spot on the basketball team, and I had been looking to my dad to provide the encouragement I needed to keep trying to earn it back. This was the man who always told me that anything was possible! And now he was telling me to give up?

"Dad," I said, "Why are you telling me to give up? You always say, 'Give your best effort! Anything is possible! Shoot for the stars!' Why is this any different? Don't you believe in me?!"

My father looked away pensively for a second before returning his focus to me.

"Ben," he said, "it's true that anything is possible, including you getting your starting spot back. And I do believe in you! But why do you need to be the one that starts? Is that really the best thing for your team? Listen, you're a great player, and I love you very much. Much, much more than Gerald Moore, who I don't know at all. But Gerald is just as good of a player as you are, and he's bigger and stronger, too, which makes a difference in basketball. Your coach decided that it's best for your team if Gerald starts. Your job in this situation is to support your team and do the best job you can as a substitute."

While I continued to stare blankly at my father, feeling more discouraged than ever, my mother filled in the silence.

"You're still a great kid, and we're still very proud that you're our son, no matter what your spot is on the basketball team. We've been talking for a long time, Ben. Why don't you go take a break from thinking about basketball for a little while, and relax?" she said.

I nodded my head at my parents and quietly walked out of the room. I had heard the words my parents were saying, but I was still in disbelief. How could a father not root for his own son? It was tough to hear my father tell me to let Gerald have the starting spot. Really tough. I still wasn't ready to give up, though. If I didn't have my parents' support, I guess I'd just have to go it alone.

Maybe not completely alone, however. I sought out my older sister, who might have some good ideas. Liz is one of the star players on her high school basketball team, and generally has good advice. Maybe she could give me some pointers on how to handle this situation.

On the door to Liz's room was a big white sign with black writing that said in all capital letters, "LIZ'S ROOM—PLEASE KNOCK." I knocked twice on the door to Liz's bedroom.

"Yes?" I heard from behind the closed door.

"It's Ben. Can I talk to you about something?" I asked.

"Just Ben? No one else?" Liz asked, her door still closed.

"Liz, it's just me. Open up," I said.

"But I heard two knocks," Liz said, then chuckled from behind the door.

Liz got a kick out of giving me a hard time.

"Liz, stop it," I said back, annoyed. "It's totally normal for one person to knock two times. Just open the door already!"

Liz opened the door, smiling, and looked down at me. I knew she was as tall as my parents, but she seemed extra tall at that moment. Maybe I felt that way because everyone kept telling me I was too small to be in the starting lineup.

"What's up, little bro?" Liz asked.

"Liz, can I talk to you about basketball? I need some help," I said.

"Sure, Ben," Liz answered. "Come into my room. What's going on?"

Liz's room had a distinct character to it. Unlike the rest of the rooms of our house, which were painted eggshell white, Liz's walls were sponge-painted lavender. Liz had done it herself last summer, when she suddenly took a strong interest in sponge painting. Liz had several sports posters hung on her walls, as well as posters of Albert Einstein and Mozart. I don't think she ever listened to Mozart's music, just that she liked the poster. In the corner of her room was her bookshelf, full with novels and sports biographies. On her top shelf were trophies she had won over the years, as well as Beh the sheep, her favorite childhood stuffed animal.

Liz might have been annoying sometimes, but deep down, she was a caring sister. I sat in her desk chair, while she sat on her bed and listened to me complain about Gerald suddenly taking my starting spot and how I didn't feel like I was important to the team anymore.

"So, how do I get my starting spot back?" I asked, after completing my monologue.

"Well, Ben," Liz said, "from what you've told me, it seems that Gerald has the same skill set and level of skill that you do, but he's a little bigger and stronger. Is that correct?"

"Yeah, but maybe more than just a little bigger," I responded.

Liz nodded. "Okay, so that being the case, I think you have two options: either reinvent yourself as a player, or take the Lou Williams route."

"Huh?" I asked, confused. "What do you mean?"

"Well, you said that Gerald plays as well as you do, but he's bigger and stronger. So...*how* exactly would you show that you should start instead of him? Instead, you have to change what your best skills are. Instead of focusing on making the best pass to your teammates, work more on catching and shooting. You'll need to become the best shooter on the team, even from long range. You'll also need to work on creating scoring opportunities for yourself off the dribble. If you can show that you're the best shooting guard on the team, then the coach will start you at shooting guard, alongside Gerald at point guard."

"But William starts at shooting guard! I can't take my best friend's spot!" I said.

"Well, I'm sure he wouldn't be happy at the beginning, but William would understand eventually. It's all part of the game, after all. There can only be five starters," Liz said.

I turned my gaze to the floor and thought about what Liz had just said. I understood her perspective, but I couldn't see myself taking my best friend's spot. True, basketball was a huge part of my life and was my favorite thing to play, watch, and talk about.

Even I could see that some things were more important than basketball, though. And friendship was one of them.

"I see you're not convinced," Liz continued. "You do have another option, as I mentioned."

"What was that, again?" I asked.

"The Lou Williams route," Liz said.

"Huh?" I asked.

"That's the same sound you made the first time!" Liz said, laughing. It seemed like she was getting a little enjoyment from my confusion. "You know Lou Williams?"

"Yeah, he's great. Great scorer."

"Lou Williams has made a career of being a sixth man. The 'sixth man' is one of the first players off the bench, and he plays a lot with the starting lineup. He can be an important part of his team's success. The NBA even has an award for Sixth Man of the Year, and Lou Williams has won it three times."

"So basically, you're telling me to just accept my spot as a backup? That's basically the same advice Dad and Mom gave me," I said, getting upset again.

"Not just to accept it, Ben, but to make the most of it. Sixth Man is an important job. NBA Legends have been the Sixth Man of the Year. Kevin McHale. Bill Walton. James Harden. Detlef Schrempf."

"Detlef Schrempf?" I asked, quizzically.

"Detlef Schrempf," Liz said with a smile. "And maybe you, too."

"Alright, Liz. Thanks for the talk. I guess I've got some thinking to do."

"My pleasure, Little Bro. Good luck!"

And with that, I got up from Liz's desk chair and walked out of her room, toward my own.

I laid down on my bed and stared at the ceiling. I had a lot to think about. I wouldn't try to challenge my best friend William for his spot, would I? But could I really accept a backup role?

I knew who I had to speak to next.

CHAPTER 9

I had to talk things over with my best friend, William Lee. We sat next to each other in English class, which often led to us getting in trouble for talking to each other. I enjoyed English, but William despised it.

Our teacher, Mrs. Fireburns, had written the objectives for our lesson on the board:

1. Review comma rules
2. Read and analyze short story

Faithful to what she had written on the board, Mrs. F began class by reviewing comma rules.

"Good morning, class. In reviewing your writing, I have noticed a lot of errors in your grammar, specifically in the area of when or when *not* to place a comma. Over the next few classes, we'll be spending significant time reviewing the rules of comma placement and practicing it in our grammar workbooks. To begin, I'm now going to write three sentences on the board without any commas at all. I want you to read them silently as I write them. Try to see where commas, if any, should be placed."

Realizing that Mrs. Fireburns would have her back turned to the class while she was writing the sentences on the whiteboard with her dry erase markers, I took advantage of the opportunity to start telling William about my quandary.

"Will," I whispered, "I need to talk to you about the basketball team."

"What?" William responded, a little louder than I would have liked him to. "About you and Gerald?"

"Shhh," I whispered back. "Yeah. Do you think I have a chance to get back into the starting lineup, or am I doomed to be a backup?"

"Umm...maybe we should save this for after class," William said back, pointing at the board.

I turned forward, looked at the board, and did a double-take. As she had promised, Mrs. F. had written three sentences on the board without commas:

1. After you write make sure you check that your commas are correct.

2. Cindy my aunt always enjoys eating her favorite dessert cheesecake.

3. Benjamin and William stop talking unless you would like
    to go to the principal's office.

By the time I finished reading, I saw Mrs. Fireburns looking at William and me with a sour expression on her face, while the rest of the class chuckled quietly.

That kept us quiet for the rest of class.

CHAPTER 10

After the bell rang to end class, I packed up my stuff and walked out of the room together with William.

"So what do you think? What should I do?" I said to William.

"I don't know," William said. "On the one hand, I like playing with you best, because you're my best friend. So I sort of wish that you would be the starter."

"Sort of wish?" I repeated back to William. "Why 'sort of'?"

William hesitated a second, before responding, "Well, it's just that, I mean, Gerald is really good. I mean, you are, too, but Gerald's size is a game-changer. I mean, he can drive right into the middle of the lane and score in traffic."

"Yeah, I know," I said. "I was speaking to Liz last night-"

"Wait, you mean Liz, the cartoon lizard from *The Magic School Bus*?" William interrupted me, with a smile on his face.

Once William got a joke in his head, it didn't pay to try to get him to stop. I just tried to go with it.

"Yeah, Liz, the cartoon lizard from *The Magic School Bus*. So anyway, I was speaking to Liz last night-"

"Hey, Dave!" William called across the hallway to Dave Jackson, a classmate of ours, who was walking in the opposite direction. "Did you know that Ben here speaks to Liz the lizard from *The Magic School Bus*? He just told me."

Dave just raised his eyebrow in curiosity and said, "I'm not even gonna ask," before he continued walking on.

William was taking this joke too far, and by this point, I was annoyed.

"Hey!" I said, "I'm trying to speak with you about something important, and you're making jokes. Stop already."

"Sorry, man," William responded, a half-smile on his face. "Just having some fun. So, what did your sister say?"

"She thought I didn't have a good chance at challenging Gerald. Her idea was that I could either change myself into a shooting guard and try to take your spot, or just settle for being a sixth man."

"Take my spot?" William repeated. "I can't give up my starting spot. I mean, you're my best friend and all, but some things are more important than friendship. Like basketball," William said with a smile, giving me a light punch in the shoulder.

"Don't worry, Will," I smiled back, "I'm not planning on taking your spot. I'm just still not happy about being a backup."

"You should be happy, though! Backups are important, too! Take Big Shot Rob, for example," William said, with a serious look on his face.

"Big Shot Rob? Very funny. Is that a cartoon character or something?" I asked, bracing myself for another joke.

"No, I'm serious. It's a nickname for Robert Horry. He played in the NBA for a lot of years, and for a good part of his career, he was a backup. He's most famous for making high-pressure shots in big moments, some of which he made even when he was a substitute," William said.

"But you're the best shooter on our team, not me," I countered.

"Horry wasn't necessarily the best shooter on his team, either," William said. "He just always seemed to be in the right place at the right time, ready to make the big shot to win the game. What I'm trying to say, Ben, is that everyone has his moment. Just because someone is a sub doesn't mean he's not important to the team, and definitely doesn't mean he won't have his time to shine. So what if you're a backup? You'll still get your time to shine. Believe me."

I nodded my head silently as I listened to what William said. I hoped William was right, because at this point, it didn't seem like I had much of a choice.

CHAPTER 11

It took a few weeks, for sure, but I eventually settled into my new role as a backup. I even became friendly with Gerald, despite the fact that he was the one who had taken my spot.

Was being a backup as much fun as being the starter? Nope. Did I get as much playing time? Of course not. Did I get to play next to my best friend, William? A little. Did I have a lot more time to think up questions to ask myself? Definitely. So that was a small benefit, I guess.

Once I took the pressure off of myself to try to take the starting spot away from Gerald, I felt more relaxed. Playing was fun again, now that it wasn't so competitive. While I always tried my hardest, if I missed a shot or made a mistake, I was able to just shrug it off and move on. I also had to admit, watching the game from the sidelines could be sort of fun, too. I became a vocal cheerleader for the team from the bench and enjoyed yelling encouragement and clapping for our players when they made a good play or were in a tense moment in the game.

Truth be told, however, there weren't that many tense moments in our games. Gerald did a great job leading the offense, and as people had predicted, he was a real difference-maker for our team. We were undefeated so far this season, having won our first seven games, and almost all of our games were won decisively, by margins of ten points or more.

I got some playing time, but it mostly came when our team was already well in the lead. Usually, I subbed in for Gerald and played alongside Allen Walker, but I also got a little time alternating with the starters. On those occasions, I played as the backup point guard alongside William, but I also got a little time at shooting guard while Gerald was playing the point. Was I on track to become "Sixth Man of the Year," like Lou Williams, as Liz had described? Not quite. Had I made any big shots, like Robert Horry? No. But was our team winning? Yes. And did I have lots of time to come up with questions to ask myself? Clearly.

Feeling less pressure as a player also meant that my mind was more open to focus on other things. I was doing well in school, and even picked up a new hobby, something I definitely never would have done during a past basketball season. I started collecting and solving all different types of Rubik's cubes. The

Classic 3 X 3 X 3, the Megaminx, the Square-1, and even the Skewb, which was my favorite, mostly because of its awesome name. After I got good at it, I would impress my friends with my ability to quickly solve a mixed-up cube. Then I'd give it to them and watch them struggle for a while, before revealing the algorithm for how to solve it.

Overall, life was good. After all, true happiness doesn't come from getting exactly what you want. It comes from learning to be happy with what you already have.

CHAPTER 12

"Hey Ben, can I talk to you for a second?" William said to me one Sunday evening, as we walked home together from basketball practice.

It was cold. I had my winter coat on, but I was still wearing my basketball shorts, and my legs were freezing.

"Yeah, what's up?" I responded. "Your legs are freezing, too?"

"Yeah, I guess," William said, "But that's not what I had in mind."

"Oh? Penny for your thoughts, sir," I said back.

"What do you mean?" William asked, confused.

I shrugged my shoulders. "I dunno," I said. "It's just something my Mom says to me sometimes when she wants to know what's on my mind."

"So does it actually involve you giving me a penny for me sharing my thoughts?" William asked. "Because I'll do that deal. I mean, I know a penny isn't a lot, but I'll take what I can get."

"My mom never gave me any money for it, so I don't think so, sorry. And honestly, you're my best friend and all, but I'm not going to pay you for sharing your thoughts with me," I said back.

"Wait a second," William said. "You just said, 'honestly, you're my best friend.' Why did you need to specify that you were saying it honestly? Does that mean that all the other times you were speaking to me, you were lying?"

"No, William, stop examining my words so closely. It's just something people say," I said back, shaking my head and wondering why William was asking me so many questions about expressions.

"Whatever," William said.

We had walked most of the way home by now and were at the point where our paths home would diverge. William needed to turn right onto Farmington Avenue, and I needed to stay straight for another few minutes. We stopped and stood on the corner for a minute to finish our conversation, like we always did.

"So anyway, what did you want to talk to me about? My legs are still freezing, so let's make this quick," I said.

"It's about Mrs. F's class. We have that test tomorrow on comma rules, and I don't know anything. I'm totally gonna fail!" William said, suddenly looking helpless.

"William, we've been working on comma rules every day in English class for last month! If you needed help, why didn't you ask for it before now? I mean, it's the day before the test, for cryin' out loud!" I said, my voice louder now.

"I'm not even going to ask what you're talking about with crying out loud," William said, before quickly continuing, "My point is, unless someone helps me on the test, I'm going to completely fail! My parents would kill me!"

"William, they're not going to kill you. Your parents are nice," I said.

"Yeah, nice until you get a bad grade. Then it's no more Mr. and Mrs. Nice Parents," William said, shaking his head with a discouraged look.

"Okay, but I'm sure they wouldn't actually kill you. And if they did, I would definitely attend your funeral. So either way, you have nothing to worry about," I said.

"Hey, I'm serious here, Ben! Fine, so maybe they won't actually kill me, but they'll definitely punish me. And who knows? Maybe I'll be forced to quit the team!" William said, near shouting now.

"The basketball team?" I asked.

"No, I mean the management team at my Dad's business, where I'm secretly the CEO," William said sarcastically, before shouting, "Yes, the basketball team, Ben!"

"So what are you planning to do about it? You can't quit the basketball team! The team needs you, and we have a real shot at the league title this year!" I said, suddenly feeling a little more concerned.

"Okay, so here's the plan. You know comma rules really well, right? I mean you've been getting everything right pretty much from before we even started our class review," William said.

"Yeah, so?" I asked.

"Well," William said, "All you need to do is let me look at your paper while you're taking the test. You don't have to move it to show it to me, or anything obvious. Just don't cover it up, so I can peek at it and make sure my answers are correct."

"William, we can't do that! It's cheating!" I said, trying to both whisper and yell at the same time.

"I know, I know," William said. "But in this situation, there's nothing to do. It's too late for me to study all the rules at this point and know them well. And if I don't get a good grade on this test, I'll probably be forced to quit the team. So what else can we do?"

"I don't know," I said. "I've never cheated before in my life."

"Really? Never ever? Not even in the tiniest way?" William asked, obviously trying to get me to find a way I had cheated one way or another.

"I don't know, man," I said. "I just know that cheating is wrong. I understand your problem, and I want to help, but I don't know if this is the way to solve it. Are you sure you can't study tonight?"

"No way," William said. "I have math homework, science homework, and I also have to finish up my social studies project. There's simply no way."

"I don't know," I said again. "I'm not sure. If you're not doing anything different anyway tonight, let me think about it, and I'll let you know tomorrow. Who knows? Maybe I'll come up with a different solution."

"I can't think of one. I'm counting on you, Ben," William said, giving me a look which made me feel guilty for not helping him.

"I'll let you know tomorrow," I said, starting to walk away. "Have a good night."

"You too, Ben," William said as he walked away.

After a few seconds of walking our own ways, I heard William shout to me again, "I'm counting on you, Ben! Don't let your best friend down!"

Gosh. What was I going to do?

CHAPTER 13

When I got home, I took a shower, ate a quick dinner with my family, then took my homework out of my backpack and sat down to work at our dining room table. The dining room wasn't really such a quiet space, but it was where my parents made me do my homework, because I usually got distracted when I tried to do it in my room. This evening, though, I sat with my homework papers in front of me on the table and my mind lost in thought about my earlier conversation with William.

I really didn't know what to do. On the one hand, I had always been taught that cheating is wrong, no matter what. To the best of my knowledge, I had never cheated myself, and I was proud of that.

On the other hand, William was my best friend, and if I allowed him to look at my paper, he wouldn't fail the test and be forced to quit the team. How could I let my best friend fail? Plus, it wasn't like I would be doing anything dishonest on my own test. William would be the one pretending to know the answers. I would just be a source of help for him.

I had been sitting in the dining room at the table for a long time when I felt my father put his hand on my shoulder.

"Hey, Ben, what's going on? You've been sitting here for at least twenty minutes already, but it looks like you haven't touched your homework," my father said. "Is something bothering you?"

"I'm dealing with a difficult moral dilemma," I said, looking first at my father, then down at the table.

"Well, you shouldn't have to deal with it all on your own," my dad said. "Would you like to speak about it with me or Mom?"

"I guess we could talk about it," I said.

From behind me, Dad walked around the head of the table and took a seat on the side opposite me. He looked me in the eyes and said, "Okay, so tell me, what's going on?"

"A friend asked me to help him cheat on our English test tomorrow. I know the material really well, and he doesn't know it well at all. He's desperate to get a good grade, and he asked me if he could look at my answer sheet during the test to make sure his answers are correct," I said.

"So, basically, you have a friend that wants to copy off your test?" my dad said back to me.

"Yeah, I know that cheating is dishonest and wrong, but I don't want my friend to fail," I said. "Plus, I wouldn't even be cheating myself. I'd just be helping him, right? Plus, it's not like anyone else would be losing out if he got a good grade, right?"

"That's quite a math problem there, with all those plusses," Dad said, with a smile.

"Dad, I'm not in the mood for jokes," I said, furrowing my brow and frowning back at him. "I need to know what to do."

"No, Ben. I'm serious," my dad said. "According to what you just said, not wanting your friend to fail, plus not cheating yourself, plus others not losing out, equals it being okay to help someone cheat."

"Well, I guess," I said.

"That's an interesting thing to say. I can tell that you're really thinking this through and trying to do what you think is the right thing," Dad said. "In fact, I think you're right. You should let your friend copy off your test. I mean, he is your friend, after all, and friends help friends."

I couldn't believe my ears. My own father was telling me to help someone cheat? He was one of the most honest people I knew! I was so bothered by what he said that I stood up from my chair as I responded.

"Are you serious, Dad? You're saying that I should cheat? How could you say that, after everything you've taught me about the importance of being honest? 'Honesty is the best policy,' you always say. 'A half-truth is a whole lie.' You always say that honesty and integrity are the most important things! And it's true that I wouldn't be cheating myself, but I would be helping someone else lie and cheat, which is wrong! You always tell us to maintain an honest reputation! I can't help someone cheat on a test, even if he is my friend!" I shouted.

At this point, I noticed that my father was looking at me with his mouth twisted into a half-smile and tears welling up in his eyes.

"I'm sorry for yelling, Dad," I said, feeling bad that I had just shouted at my father. "I'm sorry. Don't cry, Dad. I'm sorry. I just got a little confused and carried away."

My father smiled at me, and wiped the tears from his eyes before speaking.

"You don't need to apologize, Ben. I'm not crying because of the way you spoke to me, even though your tone wasn't as respectful as it usually is. I'm crying because I'm so proud of you. You have taken the values your mother and I have taught you, and you've made them your own. I'm so proud of the young man you're becoming."

"Thanks, Dad," I said, my eyes tearing up, too. What can I say? Crying is a little contagious sometimes.

"Can I have a hug, Ben?"

"Sure, Dad."

After my father and I hugged each other, I sat back down in my chair at the dining room table and looked at him.

"Wait, so you thought all along that I shouldn't show my friend my test?" I asked my dad, a little confused.

"Yeah. But I wanted to give you a chance to come to that conclusion yourself, instead of me deciding it for you. And I'm so proud you did," my dad said, smiling.

"Okay, so what should I tell my friend, though? He said he's counting on me," I asked.

"Tell William that you're sorry, but that you don't cheat and don't think he should either. He'll probably be upset at first, but he'll forgive you with time," Dad responded.

"Wait, how did you know it was William?" I asked. "I never said it was him."

"Sometimes parents just know things," Dad responded with a smile. "Besides, if you were even considering helping someone cheat, I know it would have to be your best friend. You wouldn't even consider it for anyone else."

"I guess you're right," I said. "William is normally a good kid, though. He's just desperate and worried he'll be forced to quit the basketball team if he fails."

"I understand," said Dad. "The old, 'desperate times call for desperate measures,' excuse. I don't agree, obviously, but I understand where he's coming from."

My Dad looked at the homework papers I still had to do, then looked at the living room clock hanging on the wall. It was almost 8:30.

"Okay, Ben, why don't you spend another half-hour trying to finish your homework before getting ready for bed? I'll write you a note for whatever you can't get to.

And, with my course of action determined, I started right away on my homework, quickly finished it, and went to sleep.

CHAPTER 14

It was Monday, the day of our English test.

While I had slept just fine the night before, when I woke up, I got a tight feeling in my stomach as I thought about what I was going to do. William was going to ask me desperately for help on the test, and I was going to have to tell him no. What was he going to say? Would he fail, and be forced to quit the basketball team? Was he ever going to speak to me again? For the first time in a long while, I was asking myself questions to which I had no answers.

As I walked to school by myself that morning, I tried to rehearse in my mind how I would tell William no. I thought of different versions of what I could say.

William, I can't cheat, and neither can you! So what if you fail the test? Integrity is more important!

Sorry, William, I can't help you. I don't want to risk getting in trouble and failing myself.

Sorry, William, I wish I could help you, but my parents won't let me.

Nothing I came up with was going to make William happy. I guess I had to just bite the bullet. Whatever that means.

As I neared the school entrance, I quickly concocted a plan: I would try to avoid William until third period, when we had English, and then I'd tell him right before class. Just outside the classroom, I would quickly and quietly tell him that I couldn't do it, then immediately walk into class and take my seat, so that he couldn't bother me more about it. Of course, I'd have to deal with the consequences after class, but at least there wouldn't be a way he would try to convince me or guilt me into helping him cheat before the test started.

My plan failed. Big time. Like, super big time. How? William was waiting for me at the entrance to the school building and greeted me as soon as I stepped inside.

"How's it going, Ben?" William asked, smiling and putting his arm around my shoulder and walking with me for a step, before asking, "So are we on for what we talked about yesterday?"

I ducked out from underneath William's arm, stopped walking, and turned to face him. I looked William in the eyes. Despite all my rehearsals on the way, I had trouble finding words.

"No, William," I said, pausing for a second. "I'm sorry, but I'm not a cheater, and I'm not going to help someone else cheat, either, even if he is my best friend," I said.

William's smile quickly faded and turned into a look of desperation. "Come on Ben, I'm begging you! If I don't get a good grade on this test, I'm finished! No basketball, and who knows what else my parents are going to do to me?"

That was another question I couldn't answer, but I wasn't that concerned. I mean, William's parents were really nice. I had never even heard them raise their voices before, and I had been over William's house a lot. Obviously, parents can be pretty strict sometimes, but I didn't believe William getting a bad grade would put him in any danger, and I didn't think William actually did, either.

"I'm sorry, William, the answer is no. Just do your best."

"Ben, I can't believe you're doing this to me! You're going to let your best friend fail like this? My life is going to be over!" William whined.

"Come on, Will." I responded. "It's just one test. It's not the end of the world."

"Maybe not for you," William said, frowning.

I checked my watch. We still had five minutes before we needed to be seated in our first-period classes.

59

"Listen," I said, "I'm not going to cheat, but I will give you a really quick lesson about commas. Take out a pencil, write this down, then memorize it between now and English class, and I guarantee you won't fail."

"Whatever you say, Comma Whiz," William said, taking out a pencil and scrap of paper and holding it against the wall to write.

"Okay, here goes," I said. "First of all, commas usually go wherever you'd pause in a sentence. So try reading a sentence in your head as if you were speaking, and you'll have an idea where the commas go."

"Okay," William said. "What else?"

"Remember this word: QuAILC," I said.

"*Quailk*? What in the world...?" William said back to me, shaking his head and looking at me as if I had lost my mind.

"Qu, a, i, l, c," I said. "Work with me here. If you can remember QuAILC, you can get almost all the questions right. "Qu" stands for quotation, as in someone saying something in the middle of the sentence. "A" stands for appositive, like a phrase describing something. "I" stands for introductory phrase. L stands for list, like if you have a list of nouns. C stands for combining, as in combining full sentences with a conjunction. The comma goes before the conjunction in that case.

"You're crazy, man. Tell me again. Quailk?"

"QuAILC. Qu, A, I, L, C. Quotation, appositive, introductory phrase, list, combining," I said, looking at my watch. I had less than a minute before I had to bolt to math class. Mr. Friendly was very particular about the attendance and on-time records. "Review those before English and you'll pass the test."

As I started to half-run to my first period class, William called after me.

"Ben, how do you come up with this stuff?" William asked.

How do I come up with this stuff? What can I say? It's a strange gift.

"No idea!" I yelled back. "Good luck!"

CHAPTER 15

By the time Third Period rolled around, I was confident that I would do well on the test, but I was more nervous about how William would do. I was sitting in my seat, prepared with my pencil on my desk, when William walked into the class, muttering to himself. As William sat down, he continued talking to himself, and I heard what he was saying.

"QuAILC: quotation, appositive, introductory, list, combining. QuAILC: quotation, appositive, introductory, list, combining. QuAILC: quotation, appositive, introductory, list, combining," I heard William saying to himself.

"Hey man, I think you've got it!" I said, excited.

William interrupted himself to respond, "I definitely know what QuAILC stands for. The only question is whether I understand what those things are. Tell me one last time."

I quickly reviewed it for William, and he asked me again, with a smile, "You sure you don't want to let me peek at your test, just one time at the end, to make sure I got things right?"

"I'm sure," I said confidently. "You'll be fine, though, William. You're probably not going to get an A, but you'll get through this."

Mrs. Fireburns quieted the class down and gave out the test. I looked over it. The test seemed pretty simple, just like the daily activities we had been doing at the beginning of each class. There were twenty-five sentences with no commas in them, and we were supposed to put the commas in the right places.

I was able to finish the test and check it over in about twenty minutes, but Mrs. F gave the class the whole 40-minute period to complete it. William was working until the last second, when the bell rang, and Mrs. F instructed the class to put down their pencils and hand in their tests.

I walked out of the classroom and waited by the door for William to walk out, too.

"So," I said, "How did it go? Do you think you failed?"

"Ben, all I can say is, QuAILC. If what you taught me is right, and I understood it, then I think I passed. If not, I'm in big trouble. We'll know tomorrow, when Mrs. F. hands back the tests."

The next day, Tuesday, William and I were sitting at our seats a few minutes before the start of English class. I was nervously biting my nails, and I never bite my nails! I didn't want to even think about what would happen if William failed.

"Ben?" William said.

"Yeah?" I responded.

"I just wanted to say, I'm sorry about all that stuff before," William said.

"Sorry about what?" I asked.

"You know, pressuring you to help me on the test. It wasn't right. I was just feeling a lot of pressure myself and didn't know what to do. I have to admit, no matter what grade I get on this test, I feel a lot better about not having cheated to get it. You were right the whole time. Sorry," William said, looking serious.

"It's okay," I said. "I understand. Are you nervous about what you got on the test?"

"Are you kidding me?" William said. "I haven't been this nervous since I played darts last summer with my five year-old cousin, Tim. He almost nailed me twice!"

"Who won?" I asked, smiling.

"He did," William said, shaking his head. "Don't ask."

The bell rang, and Mrs. F stood in the front of the classroom. She announced that she would be handing back the tests at the end of class.

"Oh my gosh," William said quietly, smacking the heel of his left hand on his forehead. "How am I going to survive the next 40 minutes?"

CHAPTER 16

William survived.

At the end of class, Mrs. F handed out the tests to all the students, as promised. She placed the tests on our desks face down and instructed us to turn them over and silently look at our scores. While it was a nice idea, it didn't work out exactly as she had planned.

"I got a 100!" yelled out Brian Gimpley, from the back of the class.

"We're not sharing our scores!" Mrs. Fireburns called back, with a stern look on her face.

"I got an 85. What did you get?" I heard Devin say to his neighbor on the right side of the classroom.

"An 85's not bad. I got an 87," came the response from Jessica Brown.

I flipped over my test and smiled. Like Brian Gimpley, I had also gotten everything correct and received a 100. Mrs. F had written "EXCELLENT!" in big red capital letters on the top of the page, next to the score.

I put my test back down on my desk and looked over to my left at William. His test was decorated with a good number of red marks, and William had a concerned look on his face.

"What did you get?" I asked him.

"A 76," he said.

"Okay. So, considering the circumstances, is that a good score, or a bad score?" I asked.

"I'm not actually sure myself," William replied. "It's a lot worse than I usually do, but it's definitely better than failing. My parents are not going to be happy, but it's probably not the end of the world.

"Was it really ever going to be the end of the world?" I asked William, smiling.

"I guess not," he responded, smiling back.

CHAPTER 17

While it was true that the world did not end, William did not exactly escape punishment, either. As a consequence for his bad grade, and in order to give him extra study time to address his struggles in English, William's parents made him stay home from our basketball team's practices that week. Missing basketball practice wasn't that bad of a consequence by itself, but since Coach Jones had the rule, "If you don't practice, you can't play," the fact that William was missing practice meant that he also was going to miss our next game.

William had told me the news the morning after he had brought his test grade home.

"Tough break," I said. "Sorry about that."

"Yeah," said William. "We're playing Rivercrest this week, and I was really looking forward to the game."

"I know," I said. "They're six and one so far this year, and they're one of the toughest teams in the league every year. What are we going to do without you?"

"You guys will be fine," William said. "You'll probably start in my place, and you'll do great. I'm just sorry I won't be able to play alongside you."

I wasn't convinced that I would do great. I was a point guard, not a shooting guard, and while I had definitely subbed in occasionally as shooting guard this year, I didn't feel so comfortable yet in the position. I was used to dribbling up the court and making the right passes to help others score, as opposed to moving without the ball and trying to find opportunities to score myself. However, I didn't want to make William feel any worse by telling him about my doubts. He already felt bad enough that he wouldn't be able to play in the game.

All I said was, "Yeah, we'll miss you out there."

That afternoon in practice, Coach Jones explained the situation to the team.

"Listen, guys, William's not able to practice with us this week, which means he's not going to be able to play in the game this Thursday night. Because we don't have a big team to begin with, we're only going to have seven players in this game, which means that we're all going to have to be pretty flexible with the positions we play and rotating around.

"Rivercrest is a tough team with a lot of strong players, but we have shown this year that we can take on the best teams and beat them. It's true that William has been a significant part of our success this season, but our team is greater than any individual player. We'll need everyone to give their best effort and play smart basketball, but we should come into the game confident that we can win.

"I have already given a lot of thought to our starting lineup for this Thursday night's game. We're going to keep the starting lineup the same as normal, except that Ben Taylor will play shooting guard instead of William. Ben, I know that shooting guard is not your first position, but I'm sure you're up for the challenge."

While that was pretty much what I had expected to hear from Coach, it was still very exciting to hear that I would be playing in the starting lineup again, even if it was for just one game. Exciting and nerve wracking, because I would be the one difference in our undefeated starting lineup. What if I would be the weak link whose performance would cause our team to lose our first game of the season? I didn't even want to think of the answer to that question.

As we ran our practice that day, I got extra time at shooting guard, and it felt unnatural. I wasn't comfortable, and I was too hesitant to fire up shots myself, even when I had an open shot at the basket.

After practice, Coach Jones came up to me to speak to me privately.

"Listen, Ben. I have full confidence in you. You're a natural basketball player, and natural basketball players can play any position they're put in. The position you're going to be playing next game is shooting guard. You're going to need an aggressive scoring mentality on offense. I know you can do it. Do you know that you can?"

"I think so," I replied.

"'I think so' isn't good enough," Coach Jones said. "I need you to know that you can do it. Do you know that you can do it?"

"Yessir, Coach," I said, trying to look and sound more confident.

"Okay, Ben, go home, relax, and rest up. We're going to need your best energy for tomorrow's game," Coach Jones said.

"Yessir, Coach," I said again.

I grabbed my coat and backpack, and I walked out of the gym. I would go home, but there was no way I was going to relax and rest up. I was too nervous, and I needed to prepare more for our game the next night.

CHAPTER 18

When I got home, I explained the situation to my parents and got permission to shoot baskets in my driveway with Liz. Liz graciously agreed to help give me basketball tips, as well as get my rebounds and pass them back to me, which would enable me to get in a lot more practice shots than if I had been shooting around by myself.

We had only been outside together for a few minutes when I remembered the joke William had made a while ago about me talking to Liz, the cartoon lizard from *The Magic School Bus*.

"Hey Liz?" I said, then hoisted up another shot. It hit the left side of the rim and bounced out.

"Yeah?" Liz said, catching the rebound and passing it back to me for another shot.

"Does anyone-" I shot again, this time swishing the ball through the hoop.

"Does anyone ever make a joke out of your name being the same as Liz, the cartoon lizard from *The Magic School Bus*?" I asked, as Liz passed the ball back to me.

"Oh, Ben, if I had a dollar for every time someone mentioned that cartoon lizard to me, I'd have...zero dollars. No one has ever done that to me. What makes you ask such a strange question?" Liz said, passing the ball back to me after I made another shot.

"Just wondering," I said, then shot again.

After more than two hours outside, more than 200 practice shots, and lots of advice from Liz on how to get away from my defender and score more on offense, I felt much more ready for tomorrow night's game. Would I be the star of the game? Definitely not. Would I still make mistakes? Definitely yes. Could I put in the performance our team needed from me to help us win? That remained to be seen, but I was feeling a lot more confident about it now than I had at our team practice that afternoon.

As we went inside, I tried to let Liz know how much I appreciated her time and effort.

"Thanks so much for your help, Liz. I'm feeling so much more ready for tomorrow night's game, and I couldn't have done it without you."

"My pleasure, little bro. I'm here to help." Liz smiled. "Plus, now you owe me a favor in exchange. I don't know what it is yet, but I'll let you know when I figure it out."

"Sure, Liz, whatever. I definitely owe you one," I said.

As I showered and got ready for bed that night, I tried to imagine myself playing shooting guard against the Rivercrest Wildcats. In my mind, I was sinking three-pointers, making fadeaway jumpers, and driving the lane for contested shots up close. Tomorrow evening would be the test of whether I'd be able to do all that in real life.

The next school day flew by. Sadly, I don't think I learned a thing, despite my teachers' best efforts. The whole day, my thoughts were only on the upcoming game against Rivercrest.

That evening, as our team went through our pre-game warmups, I noticed that both my parents and Liz were sitting in the stands. It wasn't unusual to have one of my parents at the game, but to have my whole family there was a treat. I guess they thought it would be a good opportunity to see me play, considering that this was the one game all season I'd be in the starting lineup.

I was nervous as all get-out. I don't even know what that means. It's just something I've heard my parents say. My best guess is that it means "really nervous". What I'm trying to say is that my whole body felt awkward, and I felt sick to my stomach.

Then I started wondering about what "sick to my stomach" means. Do people really feel sick *to* something? Don't they feel sick *with* something? But if I said I felt sick *with* my stomach, then that would be obvious. I'm always with my stomach, no matter how I'm feeling. Happy with my stomach. Sad with my stomach. Sick with my stomach. It's always there with me. Except those people who need to have stomach removal surgery. But that couldn't be the reason people say "sick *to* my stomach..."

I needed to loosen up and get my mind focused. I really shouldn't have been so nervous. Not too long ago, I had considered myself the starting point guard and one of the best players on the team! For some reason, though, this all felt like a really big deal.

I tried telling myself that it was just basketball. No matter what happened in the game, whether I played great, or terribly, or somewhere in between, it wouldn't be the end of the world. I just needed to try my best, and whatever would happen, would happen. I mean, of course it would. Whatever happens is always the thing that happens. What I meant was that it wouldn't be the end of the world. You get the point.

I noticed William walk into the gym in his school clothes. I ran over to him to ask him what he was doing at the game.

"My parents let me come to the game to support the team and to support you," William said. "Coach Jones won't let me play in the game without practicing, but I'm still allowed to come to the game."

"Cool," I said. "Any last-minute advice for me?"

"Just play your best and have fun," William responded. "Don't worry about what happens. Whatever happens, happens, and it won't be the end of the world."

"Don't even get me started," I said to William, shaking my head.

"Started with what?" William asked, confused.

"Oh, don't worry about it. I'm just glad you're here. If you have any tips during the game, let me know."

"Sure, Ben. Good luck!" William said, before walking to the bench to say hello to Coach Jones.

We finished our warm up drills, got a last-minute pep talk from Coach Jones, and lined up for the jump ball to start the game.

I was ready. *Let's do this.*

CHAPTER 19

It was the game of my dreams.

I was playing almost the whole game in a different position than I had played my whole life, and I loved it! I wasn't just sinking my shots, I was on fire! No, not actually on fire. That would have been incredibly dangerous to myself and others. I mean that I was making almost every shot I was taking.

I was following my sister's advice to move without the ball in order to get distance from my defender. Then I would get a pass and make a move to either get open for a jump shot, or drive around my defender for a closer shot in the lane. It worked over and over again, on multiple Wildcat defenders. I felt like no one could stop me.

I even shot and made two three-pointers, which I had never done before in a game. The whole experience felt surreal, like I was playing in a dream, or that I was in a video game. And while I had always enjoyed assisting others, there was a certain special feeling to scoring a basket myself and hearing the crowd clap for me. I shifted over to point guard for two short stints when Gerald had to sub out briefly, but the majority of my time was at shooting guard. And shoot, I did. I lost track of the amount of points I was scoring during the game, but I was definitely the one taking the most shots of anyone on my team.

By the time the last five minutes of the game came around, we were all exhausted from playing so much. We knew going into the game that we were all going to be playing extra minutes because we had one fewer player, but I hadn't expected to play almost the entire game. Until that point, I had sat out for only three minutes in the entire game! Allen Walker subbed in for me with five minutes left on the clock, which was good, because I had almost no energy left in my legs.

As I took my seat on the bench to watch my teammates finish the game, I looked up at the scoreboard. We were winning, 60-42 against the Wildcats.

I picked up my water bottle from underneath my spot on the bench and took a drink.

I sat back in my seat on the nearly empty bench to rest. I sure needed it.

William came over and sat down next to me on the bench.

"Ben, you were unbelievable out there! You've been on fire the whole game! We have an 18-point lead on the Wildcats! The Wildcats, Ben!"

"I know," I said. "Believe me, I surprised myself out there. Liz gave me some tips last night about moves with and without the ball, and I also took like two hundred shots, but I didn't expect to play like this. I guess something just clicked."

"Amazing. Liz, the cartoon lizard from *Magic School Bus* taught you all that?" William asked, smiling.

"William, gosh. Give that joke a rest. No one else I know makes that joke, and my sister Liz hasn't heard anyone make that joke her entire life. Her entire life!" I said back.

"Sheesh, Ben. I guess you just don't appreciate sophisticated humor," William said.

"Yeah, sure. Real sophisticated," I said back. "So, are you going to be back for practice next week?"

While we had been talking, the Wildcats were slowly cutting into their deficit, and they were now down by 14.

"Yeah," William said. "I finally learned comma rules properly and proved it to my parents, so they'll let me come back next week. I hope I'll still have my starting spot, though, after your all-star performance."

"Ha," I said. "You think Coach is going to start me over you next week because I had one great game? No way. You're our shooting guard. I'm the sixth man," I said.

"You're Big Shot Ben!" William said. "Actually, more like Big Game Ben, if we're being honest."

"William, I hope you're always being honest. We're best friends," I said, smiling.

"Hey, now you stop! I took that expression from you," William said, grinning.

We watched the end of the game together from the bench. While the Wildcats did go on a run to make it closer, mostly because our team was so tired by the end of the game, they still ended up losing, 66-58. Our undefeated Eagles team was now 8-0, and we had just decisively defeated one of the best teams in our league! Our league playoffs would be starting soon enough, and our prospects looked good. Really good.

After we shook hands with the Wildcats and wished them good game, I couldn't resist taking a peek at the scorebook before joining the team for our post-game talk with Coach Jones. I knew I had scored more points than I ever had before, but I wanted to know exactly how many.

I walked over to the scorer's table and flipped open the cover of the scorebook. The pages were paper-clipped together, so the book opened right to the record for our game. I carefully studied the page.

The scorebook listed the number of total field goals, three-pointers, and free throws made in our game, along with some other statistics. In all, I had scored 12 field goals, two of which were three-pointers, and had made all four of my free throws. Doing some quick math, I realized I had scored 30 points! I had never scored more than 14 points in a game in my whole life! I was definitely going to remember this game forever.

In our post-game huddle, Coach congratulated us on our awesome win, despite the fact that we were playing short-handed. He even gave me special acknowledgement.

"And Ben," he said, turning his gaze on me, "That was the most amazing offensive performance I have seen from anyone on the team this year. This was a team victory, for sure, but you definitely led us. You really stepped up, Ben, and you should be proud of yourself."

Hearing words like that made me feel like a million bucks. I don't mean that I felt like I was literally made up of many tall stacks of dollar bills totaling one million dollars, of course. Nor did I feel like the most enormous herd of male deer in the history of the world. It's just an expression I've heard my parents say a few times. It means you feel really important, or something like that. And on that night, I certainly did.

CHAPTER 20

As I expected, after William came back to practice, he took over the starting spot again, and things went back to how they were. Had I enjoyed my night in the spotlight? You bet I did. Did I sometimes get the feeling that I might be able to do a better job than William? Maybe a little. However, I realized that for the benefit of the team, as well as my friendship with William, it was best for things to go back to how they were.

However, while William remained the starter, I did get a few more minutes of playing time at shooting guard each game than I had before, and I tried to make the most of them. I never caught fire like I had in the game against the Wildcats, but in my mind, I was no longer only a point guard. I was now both a point guard and a shooting guard—a combo guard, if you will.

We continued to blaze through our opponents, and we finished the regular season undefeated for the first time in our school history. With the league playoffs starting soon, we were the favorites to win the championship, but there were definitely no guarantees. Eight teams qualified for our playoffs, and we would need to first win in the quarterfinal and semifinal games in order to even get to play in the championship game. There would be no doubt that every team would be playing their absolute best, as this time, each team's season was on the line.

Because of our awesome record in the regular season, we had home-court advantage in the playoffs. In the quarterfinal round, our team hosted the Woodmont Bucks, and we thrashed them, 62-39.

Our opponent in the semifinal game, the Clearwater Cougars, put up more of a fight. We were up by only four points at halftime. In the second half, the Cougars came out with a full-court press, which caught us off-guard. The Cougars took full advantage and seized the opportunity to go on a 12-4 run and take the lead by four points. For the first time in many games, we were actually trailing. It took us a while, but we eventually figured out the weak spot in their press defense, and we went on a run ourselves to retake the lead. From there on out, we controlled the game, and we ended up winning, 56-48.

With the quarterfinal and semifinal games won, we would be playing for the league championship next. Our dream season had one game left to be complete. With one more win, we would record an undefeated season. More importantly, we would bring the championship trophy home to our school for the first time.

CHAPTER 21

We had one week to practice together as a team before we played in the championship game at Midwood High School against the Rivercrest Wildcats. The Wildcats, after losing to us in the regular season, had clawed their way through their remaining opponents and the first two rounds of the playoffs. Unlike our earlier playoff games, the championship game was scheduled to be played at a neutral court with a bigger cheering section, so that more family members and fellow students could come to support their teams. Midwood had a beautiful hardwood court and huge wooden bleachers on each side of the court. They had great vending machines, too, so that was a plus.

In practice that week, Coach Jones kept pushing us hard to stick to our fundamentals, as he always did.

"Come on guys, crash the boards!"

"Box out on rebounds!"

"Put your weight on the balls of your feet on defense. Keep your feet wide!

"Slide and stay in front of him! Don't reach!"

In addition to running our same drills and practicing fundamentals, though, Coach also practiced some new offensive plays and defensive formations with us. We worked on different zone defensive formations, in addition to our regular man-to-man, as well as our full court press, which we hadn't needed to use the entire year. From the intensity of our practices, you would have gotten the impression that we were a struggling team that desperately needed to improve, rather than a team that was on the brink of an undefeated championship season.

After practice, Gerald, William and I all walked out of the gym together.

"Wow, that was crazy," I said to William and Gerald.

"I know," said William. "Haven't we proven ourselves enough this season?"

"We have," said Gerald. "but think about it. We beat the Wildcats shorthanded last game. That must have been embarrassing for them. They're going to be looking for revenge, for sure."

"True," William said, "but come on, Gerald. With you at the point, me back in the lineup, and Big Shot Ben coming off the bench, Rivercrest doesn't stand a chance. Am I right?" William said, smiling and smacking us lightly on the back.

I didn't know about Gerald, but William's logic certainly seemed correct to me.

Every practice in the week before the championship was the most intense it had been all year, and by the middle of Wednesday's practice, we were all exhausted. Seeing we were so tired out, Coach ended practice early, congratulated us on a job well done this week, and encouraged us to shoot around and just play for fun until the end of our regular practice time, which we happily did.

"Remember to arrive early to Midwood for the game tomorrow night, guys. Tip-off is at 6:30, but I want everyone there by 5:45, please."

In the kitchen that night, I told my parents about needing to get to the game early, after which I told them how excited I was for tomorrow night's title game.

"We're excited too, Ben," my dad said. "Mom, Liz and I will all be in the crowd rooting for you."

"Ben, Dad and I were speaking the other night, and we want to tell you how proud we are of you this season," my mom said.

"Why *this* season?" I asked. "Except for that one game midway through the season, I didn't really accomplish anything special."

"Well, Ben, we're always proud of you, and you're developing into a fine young man. But this season in particular, you were faced with a challenge that was bigger than an opposing defender. Losing your starting spot was a big shock to you. We're so proud that you managed to carve out a new position for yourself on the team and stay happy while supporting your teammates," Mom said.

"Thanks," I said. "This season has certainly been interesting in more ways than one. And tomorrow night will be the perfect ending."

My dad looked at me quietly for a second before responding.

"No matter what happens tomorrow in the game, we'll still be proud of you. You know that, right? No matter whether you win or lose, or whether you score 100 points or miss all your shots, we'll still be proud of you, and love you just the same," Dad said.

"Yeah, I know. I know," I said, nodding my head smiling.

My mother looked at her watch.

"Honey, it's 8:45 already. You have a big game tomorrow. Why don't you get ready for bed?"

"Sure, Mom. Love you guys. Goodnight."

"Love you, too," both my parents responded together.

And with that, I left the room.

As I laid down in my bed that night, I was expecting that thinking about the game would keep me awake. I was wrong, and quickly fell asleep.

CHAPTER 22

Despite it being the night before the big game, I slept like a baby. Definitely not like those babies who are really gassy and keep waking up because their bellies are hurting. That would have been rough. Not even like those babies who sleep well for a while, until they wake up crying in the middle of the night to eat. That would have been bad also, though I do enjoy snacks. No, I slept like a baby who sleeps the whole night without waking up. Those exist, right? If those exist, then I slept like one of those.

I went to school in the morning, but could barely focus on my classes. All people were talking about was the championship game that evening. My teammates, my classmates, even some of the teachers were talking about it. Everyone was planning on coming. It was going to be huge! I hoped there would still be snacks left in the vending machines by the time I got to them.

William and I walked home from school quickly so that we could get all ready for the game.

When I got home, I got changed, got my basketball stuff all ready, and helped set the table for an early dinner. After dinner, it was off to Midwood for the game!

Dinner was spaghetti and meatballs, my favorite. I mean, if we had a plateful of brownies for dinner, that would have been my actual favorite, but I don't really expect my mother to ever serve just brownies for dinner. Plus, if she had, there's a decent chance that once I started running up and down the court, my teammates would get a second look at what I had eaten, if you know what I mean. And if you don't know what I mean, I'm saying that I would throw up brownies all over the court.

After we cleaned up from dinner, my parents, Liz, and I got into our Corolla and drove to Midwood High. Dad pulled up to the gym entrance, and I stepped out of the car onto the sidewalk.

Mom lowered her window and called out to me.

"Ben? Since we have plenty of time, we're going to swing by the supermarket we passed to pick up some snacks for the game, okay? We'll see you in the gym before the start of the game," she said.

"But Mom," I called back, "the vending machines at Midwood are amazing! You should just get snacks from there!"

"I know, but everything costs twice as much," my mother responded. "Plus, we have plenty of time before the game starts."

"Okay, whatever. See you soon," I said, and walked toward the gym.

The gym was brightly lit, and as I remembered, the court looked stunning. They must have just polished it, because the hardwood was glimmering in the gym lights.

When I walked onto the court, it was just Coach Jones, Gerald, and John Green, our center, on our side of the court. By the time I had taken a few warm-up shots, however, the rest of our team was there, taking practice shots in our pre-game shoot-around.

We spent a long time warming up before Coach Jones called us over to the bench to give us some final words of inspiration before the game.

I looked to the crowd seating area for a moment and saw that the gym was packed! Every seat was taken, and there were plenty of people standing, too. I spied Liz and my parents sitting in the middle of the bleachers, and they waved to me. Naturally, I smiled and waved back.

"C'mon Ben, attention over here," Coach Jones said, refocusing my attention on his pregame pep talk. This time, it seemed more like a pep speech.

"Guys, you have done an amazing job all season. I'm so proud of the effort and teamwork you've demonstrated in getting here. It's hard to believe that our Eagles, who only won a little more than half their games last season, are undefeated to this point, but you have truly earned it.

"That said, we have to be on guard that we don't get overconfident. We won our last game against the Cougars, but we all know that there was a moment where the game was going in their direction and it didn't look good for us. I'm not saying that we did anything wrong there, but it's good to remember that we're not invincible.

I'm sure some of you also know about famous sports teams that seemed like they couldn't be defeated, but suffered upsets at the end. The 2007 New England Patriots played a perfect season, but lost to the Giants in the Super Bowl. The Golden State Warriors in 2016 had the best regular season record in NBA history, but lost in the NBA Finals to the Cleveland Cavaliers. The 2015 Kentucky Wildcats had an undefeated season and then lost in the Final Four.

Eagles, I believe that you are the best team in this league, I really do. We can win the championship if we go out there and give our all. But there are no guarantees. Nothing is going to be handed to you. Just like all season-long, if you want to win, you're going to have to earn it. Now let's go out there and show them what we've got!"

As I watched from the bench as the team took the court, I thought about Coach's message and wondered what the other players were thinking, as well. Coach's words made sense, but I wasn't concerned. No team had even given us a real challenge the entire season, and we had already beaten the Wildcats convincingly earlier this year, when we didn't have William's help. Were we really supposed to be worried that they could beat us now, with our team at full strength? I, for one, didn't think so.

CHAPTER 23

John Green won the tipoff to start the game, and Gerald Moore recovered the ball, before taking it up the court. Gerald threw a bounce pass to William, who fired a quick shot that rimmed out. The Wildcats center leapt and caught the rebound, then threw a quick outlet pass to the point guard, who sprinted down the floor for a three-on-two fast break.

After two quick passes, the Wildcats made an open layup to score the first two points of the game. Then the Wildcats really caught us by surprise by using their full-court press. Their point guard, shooting guard and small forward swarmed as we tried to inbound the ball. The Wildcats stole the inbounds pass and scored another layup to go up 4-0.

The Wildcats stayed in their full-court press after their basket, cutting off the passing lane to Gerald. When William broke free and caught the inbounds pass from Josh Martin, he tried to dribble up court, but was quickly trapped by two Wildcats. Stuck, William hurled a pass down court, which was picked off by the Wildcats power forward, who passed it to the point guard to start their offense again.

The game continued like that for the first few minutes, and the Wildcats built an 8-0 lead on four straight baskets.

Coach Jones called timeout and drew up a play for us to beat their full-court press. Our center would inbound the ball, and Gerald would quickly cut to the sideline, while William would go up the middle of the court, and Michael Lopez would come down from midcourt to offer help if necessary.

The play wasn't needed, however. When our team came out of our huddle to pass the ball inbounds, the Wildcats had already stopped pressing and had set up in a half-court defense.

Now we really could get to work. Our team slowly cut into the Wildcats' lead, simply by playing smart offense and tough defense. The fact that we were behind on the scoreboard didn't bother us. We had been behind in the last game, too, and ended up winning convincingly.

With about ten minutes left to go in the first half and our team down by five points, 20-15, I subbed into the game for William. Gerald Moore stayed at the point, Allen Walker was at small forward, Kevin Levine was at forward, and John Green was still at

96

center. As I stepped onto the court, the memories of my amazing performance earlier this season came rushing back to me, and I smiled. Who knew what I would accomplish in this game? Maybe I'd take over on offense again and be the hero for our team!

Kevin Levine passed the ball inbounds to Gerald, who slowly dribbled the ball up the court, and I jogged up ahead of them to my offensive position on the right side. As I was running, I was joined by a taller defender, who I didn't initially recognize.

"Hi," I said to the guy wearing jersey number 14. "I'm Ben. What's your name?"

"You can just call me your worst nightmare," the boy answered.

Worst nightmare? How nice, I thought. *Who taught this guy his great manners?*

"I was injured on the bench the last time our teams played together, but I was watching your moves. Hope you enjoyed scoring last game, because you won't be doing any of it tonight," he continued.

"Well, pleased to meet you, Mr. Nightmare, and wishing you best of luck this evening," I said back to him, smiling. We would all soon see if he could back up his trash talk.

I made a v-cut to get some space from my defender, and Gerald passed the ball to me. I kept the ball moving by passing it down to John Green in the post. John pivoted to his right, took two dribbles in while tightly guarded, then spun and banked a shot off the backboard and in, cutting the Wildcats' lead to three.

The Wildcats center passed the ball inbounds to their point guard, who brought the ball up the court. The point guard passed the ball around the perimeter of the three point line. As the ball was being passed back to my man, I stepped in front of the pass, knocked it forward, and started streaking down the court. It was a one-on-zero fast break. I had only empty court in front of me. I coasted as I went up for the layup, and...

THWACK!

My shot was smacked out of bounds from behind.

"Out of bounds! Gold ball!" the referee said, pointing in the direction of our basket.

As I looked behind me to see who had blocked my shot, I saw that it had been Nightmare that had chased me down. *Gosh. That guy.*

Almost as if on cue, he glared at me and said in a low tone, "Like I said. Your worst nightmare."

The referee handed the ball to Kevin, who passed it in, and then I caught a pass from Gerald. I needed to make a move and score on Nightmare to quiet him down. I head-faked to my left, then drove to my right. Nightmare stayed with me, forcing me to lob a difficult shot over his outstretched hand. I missed, and the

98

Wildcats got the rebound and started up the court in the other direction.

The Wildcats missed a jump shot on their end, and we came back down the court. This time, when I caught a pass from Kevin Levine, I gave a jab step as if I was going to drive in, then stepped back for a jumper just inside the three-point line. Nightmare leapt and tipped my shot to block it, and it landed in the hands of the Wildcats center.

Gosh, that guy really is my worst nightmare, I thought, as I ran back on defense.

After being shut down three times, I gave up trying to score myself and just tried to help my teammates by making good passes.

Soon, William checked back into the game, and I moved over to point guard. Our teams played evenly for the next several minutes, and by the time I checked out of the game with a few minutes left to go in the half, we were still down by three points.

I noticed that when I left the game, Nightmare did, too. Was he in the game just to guard me? It sure seemed like it.

The buzzer for halftime sounded, and I looked at the scoreboard. Wildcats 31, Eagles 29. We were still down by two, with one half of the game left to go. At this point, it was any team's game to win, but we were all pretty surprised that we hadn't already locked up the game already, as we had done many times during the regular season and playoffs.

After he let us get drinks of water, Coach Jones reminded us to keep giving our best effort.

"Keep plugging away, guys, he said. "This is shaping up to be a fight until the end. We're going to start the second half with the same players that started the game, and we're going to play an up-tempo offense to score some quick points and jump out to a lead. Gerald, William and John all have two fouls already. Keep playing tough defense, guys, but be careful with those fouls. Okay, Eagles on three."

We huddled into a circle, put our hands in the middle, and said, "One, two three, Eagles!" and the starters walked back onto the court.

Coach took me aside as I was heading toward the bench.

"Hey, Ben, it seems like the guy who was guarding you was sent in just to cover you. A Ben-specialist, of sorts," Coach said.

"Yeah, I noticed that, too," I said.

"Well," Coach said, "that guy seems to know all your moves. If you want to get by him, you're going to need to come up with some new ones. I can also tell our centers to set some more screens for you up high so that you can get some more separation from him. Maybe that will help."

CHAPTER 24

As Coach suggested, our starters came out running, which caught the Wildcats a little off guard, especially since they didn't have all their starters on the court to begin the second half.

We quickly tied the game on a post-up move from John Green. Soon after, a mid-range jump shot from William gave us a two-point lead. With us in front for the first time in the game, 33-31, the Wildcats coach called timeout and subbed in his starters before we could extend our lead any more.

After the timeout, the teams played pretty much evenly. We traded baskets for a while. Then, both teams struggled to score for a stretch, probably due to tiredness. Along the way, our starters had picked up more fouls and were at risk of fouling out of the game. Currently, William and John Green each had four fouls, and Gerald and Josh Martin both had three. Any player that reached five fouls in the game would foul out and be disqualified from playing the rest of the game.

With 10 minutes left to go in the second half, Coach Jones signaled to me to come over to him from my spot on the bench. When I got there, he began speaking to me, but kept his eyes on the game being played in front of him.

"Ben, I need you to go in there and provide an offensive spark for our team. I'm putting you in for William at shooting guard. I know what's-his-name was shutting you down earlier—"

"Yeah, Nightmare."

"What?" Coach turned to me, confused.

"Never mind," I said. "So I need to find a way to score?"

"Yes," said Coach. turning back to the game. "Remember, he seems to know all your moves, so if you're going to get past him, you're going to have to try something new. Good luck. We're counting on you."

"Okay, Coach," I said quietly, nodding my head, but cringing on the inside. *They were counting on me to score on Nightmare?*

"Walker, Levine! At the next substitution, you guys and Taylor are going in for Lee, Lopez and John. Bring some energy, guys! We need it!"

Allen and Kevin got up from the bench and joined me at the scorer's table.

"Foul! Gold, Number 32! Two shots!"

Michael Lopez had just picked up his third foul, trying to block a Wildcat layup. The Wildcat forward missed the layup attempt, but would get to take two foul shots from the free throw line.

Seeing us waiting to enter the game, the referee blew his whistle, the scorer's table sounded the buzzer, and we entered the game. I jogged onto the floor with Kevin and Allen, and I patted William on the back and told him I was subbing in.

William looked at me and smiled as he said, "Go get 'em, Big Shot Ben. You got this," before turning and jogging off the floor.

I hoped he was right, but I wasn't so sure.

The Wildcats player sank his first free throw, putting them up by one, 42-41.

My brain was racing with ideas for things I could do differently to shake Nightmare on the offensive end. I definitely wasn't the most creative player offensively, but I was trying to think of little changes I could make to the moves Liz had taught me to throw Nightmare off.

The Wildcats forward missed his second free throw, and Kevin Levine got the rebound. He passed it to Gerald, who slowly brought the ball up the court as we all ran to set up into our offensive positions.

Gerald passed the ball to Kevin Levine at the elbow of the free throw line, who passed the ball back out to me at the three point line. As I stared into Nightmare's face, I thought about what Coach had said. *If you're going to get past him, you're going to have to try something new.*

I dribbled forward once with my left hand, then hopped back as if I was going to shoot a step-back jumper like Liz had taught me. This time, though, instead of shooting, I faked a shot.

Fooled, Nightmare jumped toward me to block my shot. Once he was already flying in my direction, I hurled a shot up, crashing into Nightmare in the process, and falling down to the court. The shot missed badly, but the referee blew his whistle, which was actually what I had been going for. "Foul, Green Number 25. Three shots."

I heard our fans cheering as they realized I had been fouled while shooting from behind the three-point line and would get the opportunity to shoot three free throws instead of the normal two. If I made all three, our team would again be up by two, with less than ten minutes to play in the championship game.

"Let's go, Ben!" I heard William yell from the bench. "Big shots!"

The teams lined up in their spots on the sides of the lane. I lined up at the foul line and tried to take some deep breaths. The pressure was on, and I knew that all the eyes in the gym were on me. Considering how many people were in attendance, that definitely meant hundreds of eyeballs.

The referee gently bounced the ball to me, put his thumb and index finger together in a circle, and held up his remaining three fingers.

"Three shots," the ref announced.

My heart was beating quickly and my muscles felt tight. The gym air around me felt extra thick. I closed my eyes, inhaled deeply, and then exhaled. I stared at the basket for a second and then went into my free throw routine. Dribble the ball once. Catch it. Adjust my hands on the ball. Bend my knees slightly and shoot.

Swish!

Our fans erupted in cheering with the first free throw I made, and I felt all the pressure melt away. After the first made free throw, I suddenly had confidence that I would make the next two as well. The referee again bounced me the ball, and I went back into my free throw routine. Dribble the ball once. Catch it. Adjust hands on the ball. Bend knees. Shoot.

Swish!

The crowd cheered again, and I think I heard Liz from the stands yell, "Way to go, Ben!"

For the third time in a row, the referee passed me the ball, and I followed my free throw routine. I shot and swished my third consecutive free throw. William was right. Big shots, indeed!

The crowd cheered much louder this time, and I couldn't help but smile. We were up, 44-42, and I felt like I was finally waking up from my Nightmare.

The Wildcats passed the ball in, and we ran back on defense. I was guarding Nightmare, who didn't seem like much of an offensive threat. As the Wildcats worked the ball around their offensive end, I took two steps back in toward the middle of the court in order to provide help defense if needed.

The Wildcats small forward pump faked Allen Walker, then drove around him to the right. Seeing that he was driving the lane for a shot, I came over from the other side of the court, and as the Wildcats player jumped to shoot, I stuck my hand out and blocked his shot from behind.

FWEET!

The referee's whistle blew, signaling a foul.

"Foul, Gold, Number 3. Two shots!"

I couldn't believe it! I had blocked the shot cleanly, touching nothing but the ball, and the ref had called me for a foul! My eyes felt like they were going to bug out of their sockets, and I felt hot all over. I looked toward Coach to show him my frustration with the referee's call. Coach Jones just nodded and held up his hands to signal to me to calm down.

The truth is, it really doesn't do any good to argue with the referees in youth basketball. In the NBA, the referees have to put up with the star players complaining about how they were fouled or didn't actually foul someone. In our youth league, if a player starts to complain about a call, the referees will almost immediately call a technical foul, giving the other team an additional two free throws and possession of the ball. Frustrating as it was, it definitely didn't pay to argue. And as Coach always tells us, referees are people, too. Even though they sometimes make mistakes, they still need to be treated with respect. But did the ref really need to make a mistake at this point in the game?

As I stood behind the three-point line, watching the Wildcats forward prepare to shoot his free throws, I refocused on what I had to do next. If he made both of his shots, the game would be tied again.

The Wildcats player clanged his first shot off the front rim, but made the second. We were still up by one, and by this point, I had a cool head and was focused on what I needed to do to help our team win.

Kevin Levine inbounded the ball to Gerald, who brought the ball up and passed it to me, standing in the top right corner of the three-point line. I caught the ball, pump faked, then dribbled to my right. Nightmare didn't fall for the fake this time and stayed with me. I passed the ball over to Walker, who fed the ball to Josh Martin, who passed the ball back to Gerald, who threw it to me.

This time, when I caught it, I drove left, then did a crossover dribble through my legs to my right side, then dribbled back to my left, and then crossed over again to my right, switching directions each time. I got Nightmare so crossed up that he tripped and fell backward onto his rear end. With Nightmare on the floor, I dribbled in two steps to my right and shot a floater over the Wildcats center who was rushing out to guard me.

Swish!

Our crowd went wild over the whole thing, and I couldn't suppress my smile as I ran back on defense. I had never crossed anyone up like that before, and I had certainly never made anyone fall down. In fact, I don't think I had seen anything like that before, except in highlight videos. It was a shame that such a pretty move only counted for two points.

The Wildcats brought the ball up the floor, trailing by three, 46-43, with only a little more than seven minutes left in the game. On defense, I crept toward the middle of the court again, leaving Nightmare more open. Considering that he had scored zero points to this point in the game, I figured he wasn't one of their main scorers, and that my defensive efforts would be most valuable in helping my teammates.

The Wildcats worked the ball around their offense, and I crept closer and closer to the middle, farther away from Nightmare. I had a feeling that they were about to work the ball inside to one of their big men, and I was more than ready to double-team.

Considering how open I had left him, I guess I shouldn't have been surprised that they passed the ball to Nightmare, standing wide-open at the three-point line, ready to launch a shot. If he made the three-pointer, it would tie the game. I charged at him from the middle of the court and leapt to contest his shot, but I came nowhere close to blocking it.

Nightmare's shot was straight on, but clanged off the back rim. Since I had been running out to block the shot, I continued sprinting up the court, a few steps ahead of everyone. Gerald had caught the rebound, and hurled it down court to me. I had to slow down a bit, but managed to catch the ball over my left shoulder like a football wide receiver. I dribbled toward the basket for a layup, which would put us up by five, a good lead, with only seven minutes left in the game.

I jumped up off my left foot and raised my hand toward the basket, but to my great dismay, once again had the ball smacked out of bounds. This time, I didn't need to turn around to know who had made the defensive play, but when I did, I saw Nightmare smiling back at me.

"Got you this time, Taylor," he said, with a grin. "Your moves were nice while they lasted. Too bad it's over for you now."

I wasn't so sure.

CHAPTER 25

The out-of-bounds ball stopped the game clock and allowed the teams an opportunity to make substitutions. For our Eagles, William came back into the game and Gerald subbed out, which meant that I would be playing point guard. John Green came in at center, subbing out Josh Martin and moving Kevin Levine to power forward.

Gerald and Josh had played for thirteen minutes straight, and were both really exhausted. They slowly jogged off the court and sat down next to Michael Lopez on the bench, who I imagined would be subbing back in soon.

Kevin Levine tried to inbound the ball to Allen Walker, but the Wildcats defender tipped the pass, which then bumped off Allen and went out of bounds. Since the last touch was made by Allen, it would be Wildcats ball. Bummer.

We ran back on defense, and I now guarded the Wildcats point guard instead of Nightmare, who himself had subbed out at the last dead ball. The Wildcats moved the ball around quickly on offense, before their center banked in a turn-around shot from the right low block, cutting our lead to only 46-45.

We played for a few more minutes without either team scoring a basket. Both tired teams were settling for jump shots instead of driving the ball to the basket, and the shots were off. With three minutes left to play, we were still clinging to our one-point lead. When we got possession of the ball, Coach Jones called timeout to plan out the last few minutes of the game.

"Listen, Eagles. This has been our toughest game of the season, and it's not over yet. Everyone needs to stay alert out there and keep up the high-energy play. Don't just settle for jumpers. If we get down by more than two at any point, I'm going to signal to you to go into our full-court press, and you'd better expect the same from the Wildcats if we're ahead in the final minute. If they do press, remember the play we drew up in the first half. Use that.

I'm sending back in the starters to finish out the game. Ben, Allen, and Kevin, you guys did a tremendous job out there, and I'm proud of all of you. Okay, guys, let's stay strong for the final three minutes and bring the championship home to Ridgeview. On three, let's go Eagles."

We put our hands in the middle and loudly chanted, "One, two, three, Eagles!" and raised our hands up in unison.

The starters from both teams took the floor, and the crowds from both sides were cheering. Who would have thought that the team we dominated earlier in the year would have given us such a challenge in the championship game?

We inbounded the ball, and Gerald immediately made a dribble move on his defender and drove into the lane. He rose up and shot a floater off the center pane of the backboard, which beautifully swished through the hoop.

Yes! The basket put us up three again, 48-45.

The Wildcats guard brought the ball up the court, and passed the ball inside to their center, who had posted up on John Green. With four fouls, and in danger of fouling out, John tried to hold his ground, but couldn't play defense as aggressively as he normally would. Their center spun left and hoisted a hook shot, which missed.

As Josh Martin pulled down the rebound, William sprinted down the right sideline. Josh hurled a one-handed baseball pass in his direction, but it was picked off by the Wildcats shooting guard, who was trailing two steps behind William. The shooting guard brought the ball up the court and passed the ball to the point guard, who continued moving the ball around the offense by passing to the power forward.

Trailing the play, William sprinted back and caught up to guard the shooting guard. However, just moments later, the Wildcats point guard set a screen on William, enabling their shooting guard to run by and get open space at the top of the three-point line. Gerald noticed the pick a little late, and while he tried to switch onto the shooting guard, the Wildcats guard was still able to get off a clean three-pointer.

It was a high-arching shot, and everyone watched as the ball bounced off the front rim, then the back rim, then the front rim again, and through the hoop. With a clutch three-pointer, the Wildcats had just tied the game at 48, with just under two minutes left to play.

The game was now tied, and with the dramatic steal and three-pointer, it felt like momentum was shifting in the Wildcats' direction. I shot Allen and Kevin a nervous look on the bench, and they seemed pretty uneasy themselves. The confidence we had all felt before the game, and that I had felt personally after I had made my three free throws just minutes before, was now gone. In its place was the realization that this game was anyone's to win, and a lucky bounce or two might determine the end of what had until this point been our team's best season in memory.

Gerald brought the ball up the court and passed the ball to William, who jab-stepped to his left and drove right. The defender beat William to the spot where William was driving, and stood his ground as William crashed into him, sending the Wildcats defender falling backward. The referee blew his whistle to call a foul.

FWEET!

"Foul! Gold, number 23! Green ball!"

The referee placed one hand behind his head and pointed in the opposite direction down the court, and we realized that William had just been called for an offensive charging foul. It was William's fifth foul, and he had just been disqualified from the game.

"Ben, you're in for William," called Coach Jones. "Go get 'em."

I ran onto the court and patted William on the back, who was slowly walking off the court while shaking his head in disbelief. I don't know if he was upset about his own decision to make that move, or whether he disagreed with the referee's call, but he was so upset that he didn't say anything to me as he walked off the floor. I tried not to take it personally.

Interestingly, as William came out and I came in, the Wildcats substituted out their starting shooting guard and brought in Nightmare. I was surprised that with the score tied, they thought it was more important to stop me from scoring than to have one of their own better scorers on the court.

The display on the scoreboard showed 1:32 left in the game, and that the score was tied at 48. The Wildcats inbounded the ball with a chance to take the lead at this critical moment.

As the Wildcats brought the ball up the court and worked the ball around their offense, we remained tough in our half-court defense, and didn't give anyone room to shoot or drive. After a while, they seemed to lose patience, and the Wildcats power forward forced up a difficult jump shot that clanged off the front rim. Their center grabbed the offensive rebound and jumped to shoot a layup.

John Green jumped to block his shot, which resulted in good news and bad news. The good news was that their center missed the shot. The bad news was that the referee called a foul on John, which like William, was his fifth foul, removing him from the game.

Coach Jones rested both his hands on his head as he stared onto the court. Our best scorer, William, had fouled out some moments ago, and now our best big man, John Green, had also fouled out. To make matters worse, the Wildcats center would be taking a trip to the free throw line to potentially take the lead for his team with just 56 seconds left to play in the game. Things were not looking good for the Eagles.

Kevin Levine ran onto the court as John jogged off of it. The players lined up at their spots along the sides of the key, as the

Wildcats center stepped to the foul line and took a deep breath. He was understandably nervous. These were likely some of the most significant free throws he had ever taken in his life.

The referee bounced the ball to the Wildcats center, who dribbled twice, spun the ball in his hands, bent his knees, and shot.

Swish!

A huge cheer rang out from the Wildcats crowd after their center's first made free throw, and his teammates briefly walked up to him to give him high fives before returning to their spots for the second free throw.

The center's second free throw swished through the hoop, and he pumped his fist in celebration. I looked up at the scoreboard, though I didn't really need to. The Wildcats were up 50-48, with just 56 seconds left to play.

Michael Lopez inbounded the ball, and Gerald brought it up court at a relaxed pace, despite the ticking clock. The truth was, we needed to stay composed and under control to have a chance to win the game, so while it might have appeared that Gerald seemed too relaxed under the circumstances, it wasn't necessarily a bad thing.

As Gerald neared the midcourt line, we heard Coach Jones yelling from the bench.

"Green beans! Green beans!"

While the Wildcats briefly shot each other confused glances, our team had gotten Coach's message. Coach had told us in practice that week that if he wanted to call an isolation play, in which the rest of our team would clear out of the way so that one of our players would have space to try to make a move on his defender, he would call out the name of a food that began with that player's name. Green beans of course, begins with the letter g, which meant that Gerald was nominated for the play.

I couldn't imagine a bigger moment in our season. The championship was on the line, we were down by a basket, and we desperately needed to score to stay in the game. Basically, our hope was to score on this possession to tie the game and stop the Wildcats from scoring on their next trip down the floor. Then, with both of us tied as the game clock expired, we would play an overtime period, where we'd hopefully take the lead and win the game. An even more unlikely possibility is that we could get a defensive stop on the Wildcats and then score another game-winning basket, but that was basically hoping for a miracle. None of it would be possible, however, without scoring a basket now.

Gerald dribbled the ball from center court to the left side, pausing briefly around the three-point line, all the while guarded by his defender. The rest of our team spaced ourselves out on the right side of the court.

I glanced at the game clock and saw that there were now 46 seconds left in the game. I really shouldn't have looked, because we all had to be ready in case Gerald got stuck and needed to throw an emergency pass to one of us.

Gerald dribbled to his right, then left, then right again, and drove to the basket. Gerald was able to get by his defender by a step, and pulled up for a running shot in the middle of the lane before the other Wildcats were able to converge on him.

Gerald's shot bounced off of the rim and out to the right side. Josh Martin quickly grabbed the offensive rebound and shot the ball off the backboard and in, scoring two points for our team!

Josh's clutch rebound and putback had just tied the game, 50-50. The gym was roaring now, with both sets of fans cheering for their teams.

As we ran back to set up in our defense, I noticed that an important member of our team wasn't with us. Gerald was sitting on the other end of the floor, clutching his ankle. He must have injured it when he came down from his shot.

The referee blew his whistle to stop the game clock at 41 seconds, and Coach ran onto the floor to help Gerald. After a little while, Gerald was able to get up with a little help, hobbled off the court, and took a seat on the bench. Allen Walker checked into the game, and I moved to point guard.

With William and John Green having fouled out, and Gerald now injured, we were down to our five remaining players to finish the game, and we were without our three strongest offensive players.

With just 41 seconds to go and the score tied, we expected the Wildcats to hold the ball for as long as they could before shooting, so as to leave us as little time as possible to score once we got the ball back.

Out of timeouts, Coach Jones yelled to us from the sidelines.

"Tough defense! Not too aggressive, though! Make them earn their shot!"

The Wildcats lined up around the perimeter of the court and passed the ball from one player to another to run down the time on the game clock. While they had begun by passing with crispness and accuracy, as they saw that we were not challenging them, their passes became a little more relaxed.

As the ball moved away from my area on the court, I looked up at the game clock, which now read 25 seconds, and thoughts raced through my head. Whether or not the Wildcats scored, what were the chances that we would be able to score on a last possession with our top three scoring threats out of the game? It was possible, but the odds were against us. I imagined that I might be the first option of the remaining players, but I didn't trust myself to score against Nightmare under pressure.

Thinking quickly, I came up with an idea. If my plan worked, we would take a big step toward winning the game. If it failed, we'd almost certainly find ourselves in a big hole. A hole perhaps too big to dig out of.

As the Wildcats passed the ball back in my direction, I leapt into the passing lane just in time to deflect the ball and knock it forward. I chased after the ball, caught up to it mid-bounce, and began dribbling as fast as I could down the court.

The crowd cheered as I sprinted down court to attempt a layup.

As I got closer to the basket, I saw out of the corner of my eye that someone was chasing me. I didn't need to see him, really. Nightmare had been all over me all game.

It was at that moment that I realized that my brilliant idea to steal the pass might not have been so brilliant, after all, if Nightmare blocked my shot. For half a second, I thought about giving up on the layup attempt, setting up our offense, and holding the ball for the last shot. But what would happen if we missed that shot and went into overtime? Could we really beat the Wildcats in an overtime period, considering we only had five players available? That would be near impossible. We had to capitalize on the opportunity and try to win the game now.

I heard Coach's voice echoing in my head. *That guy seems to know all your moves. If you want to get by him, you're going to need to come up with some new ones.*

By now, Nightmare was right behind me. I knew that he was going to leap to block my layup, like he always did. If I wanted to score, I had to do something new. But what?

I got close to the basket, picked up my dribble, lifted my outside foot slightly, and raised my right arm as if going for a layup. However, I didn't jump off the ground, and as my arm got higher, I moved my hand to the top of the ball to stop myself from shooting it. It was a risky move, but I was trying to fake out Nightmare.

I glanced behind me, and Nightmare was in the air, coming toward me! He had fallen for the fake!

I leapt straight up and into Nightmare. Pushed by the impact of our collision, I threw up a really strong shot before falling to the floor.

The referee blew his whistle to call the foul on Nightmare, which is exactly what I was going for. The basketball bounced off the back rim, then the left rim...and fell out.

Our fans let out a collective groan at the sight of my shot falling out, and I was disappointed, too. But I would still get two shots from the free-throw line to give my team the lead.

As we lined up at the foul line, I heard William yell out, "Let's go, Big Shot Ben!"

I flashed William a smile on the bench and shook my head. A little embarrassing, but what can you do? He's William, after all.

As the players lined up on the sides of the key, and I lined up at the foul line, I felt the weight of the game on my shoulders and tightness in my chest. These shots could potentially be the winning points for my team! I looked at the game clock. There were 18 seconds left. Even if I made the shots, we'd still have to get another stop on the defensive end to prevent the Wildcats from tying it up. But first I needed to make the shots, or we might just be handing the ball right back to the Wildcats with a chance to win.

The referee bounced me the ball. I took a deep breath, but I just didn't feel right. I began my free throw routine. *Dribble the ball once. Catch it. Adjust my hands on the ball. Bend my knees slightly and shoot.*

The ball went up bounced off the back rim, then the front rim, then out.

To my great dismay, the unlucky bounce kept the score tied as my final free throw shot approached.

Our fans let out a groan as the ball rimmed out, and the Wildcats crowd cheered, which didn't exactly help me feel any better.

The referee handed me the ball for my second shot. I took another deep breath to calm myself down. I dribbled, then caught the ball. I adjusted my hands, bent my knees, and shot.

The ball hit the back rim and bounced out, right into the hands of Josh Martin! Josh passed the ball to Michael Lopez, who passed the ball back to me, and we quickly got into our offensive set. The clock stood at 16 seconds, and was ticking down.

"Babaganoush! Babaganoush!" Coach Jones called out from the bench.

It took me a second to realize that Coach wasn't calling for someone to bring him a Mediterranean eggplant dish. He was using his code for me, Ben, to run an isolation play on my defender. My worst Nightmare.

I dribbled to the left side of the court, and my teammates went to the right. At this point in the game, we were definitely holding the ball for the final shot. That way, even if I missed, we would still go into overtime, instead of giving them a chance to win before time ran out. I dribbled until the clock ticked down to eight seconds and then started to make my move. I dribbled hard to my right, then planted my left foot, spun around to the left side, stepped back, and shot.

I watched the ball float toward the basket. It felt like things were going in slow motion.

The move I just made had given me space to get my shot off, but it had thrown me off balance, and my shooting mechanics off-kilter.

The basketball gently hit the right side of the rim and dropped through the basket.

The ball had gone in! It went in! We were winning, 52-50!

Our crowd let out a massive cheer, and I looked at the clock, which had stopped with two seconds remaining. Two seconds was technically enough time for the Wildcats to get off a shot. We couldn't celebrate just yet.

Our team ran back on defense, ready to intercept a long pass attempt coming from the Wildcats baseline.

The Wildcats inbounded the ball to their point guard, who took one dribble forward and shot the ball from behind the jump ball circle at center court. The ball soared through the air and missed the basket badly. Nothing but air.

Our crowd started cheering again, and the disappointed Wildcats walked back to their team bench to speak to their coach.

I looked over to where my parents and Liz had been in the stands. All three were cheering. My mom caught my eye and blew me a kiss. Liz shook her fist above her head in celebration and cheered. My dad was clapping, and I noticed he was crying, too, with a big smile on his face. Seeing him made me cry a little, too.

William and John Green ran to join us on the court, and Gerald, helped by Coach Jones, slowly hobbled over to where we had formed a team mob, close to center court.

William turned to me and yelled, "I told you, Big Shot Ben! I told you! Everybody has his moment! You're the hero!"

I looked at William and smiled. I didn't fully agree with him. My last basket was only one small contribution to our team's victory, which was earned because of our whole team's steadfast effort and determination throughout the forty-minute game. Every player on our team had made his best contribution to bring us to that final moment. I was simply the one fortunate enough to have the opportunity to score the game's last two points. I didn't feel like I should be celebrated any more than Josh Martin, Gerald, William, John, or any of our other players.

Still, "Big Shot Ben" does kind of have a nice ring to it...

DISCUSSION QUESTIONS

1. What lessons did Ben learn over the course of the story?

2. If you were Ben, what would you have done differently?

3. Which character in the book are you most like, and why?

4. What does a person need in order to be happy?

M. L. SHOCHET is a writer, teacher, and father, who has lived in five different U.S. states and two countries. He is the author of wholesome-stories.com, and enjoys writing stories that are fun for his readers, with content that parents can feel good about, too. When he is not writing or teaching, he loves learning and spending time with his family.

ALSO FROM M.L. SHOCHET

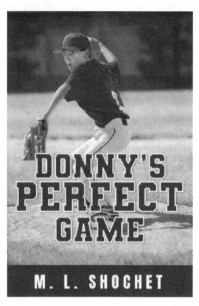

Donny was the league's best pitcher...until he suddenly lost it all. Now Donny can't get control of his pitches, and instead of helping his team win, he's bringing them down.

Will Donny ever regain his control and help his team win, or is he destined to remain a wild pitcher forever? Join Donny as he overcomes obstacles on the mound, troubles in math class, and playing alongside his archrival...on his quest to pitch the perfect game!

FOR EVEN MORE, PLEASE VISIT
www.wholesome-stories.com

HELP SHARE THIS BOOK WITH OTHERS!

If you liked this book and think others might as well, here are things you can do to help readers find out about me and my books:

1. Lend your copy out to your friends, or just tell them about it!

2. Buy a friend a copy of the book for his or her birthday!

3. Donate a copy of the book to your school or local library.

4. Ask your parents to recommend my book on social media or "like" the wholesome-stories.com Facebook page (www.facebook.com/wholesomestories).

5. Ask your parents to post a review on the book's Amazon.com page to let others know that you liked it.

THANK YOU!

Made in the USA
Middletown, DE
27 June 2022